sweetest kiss

BOOK THREE OF THE REBEL COURT

sweetest kiss

ALIANNE DONNELLY

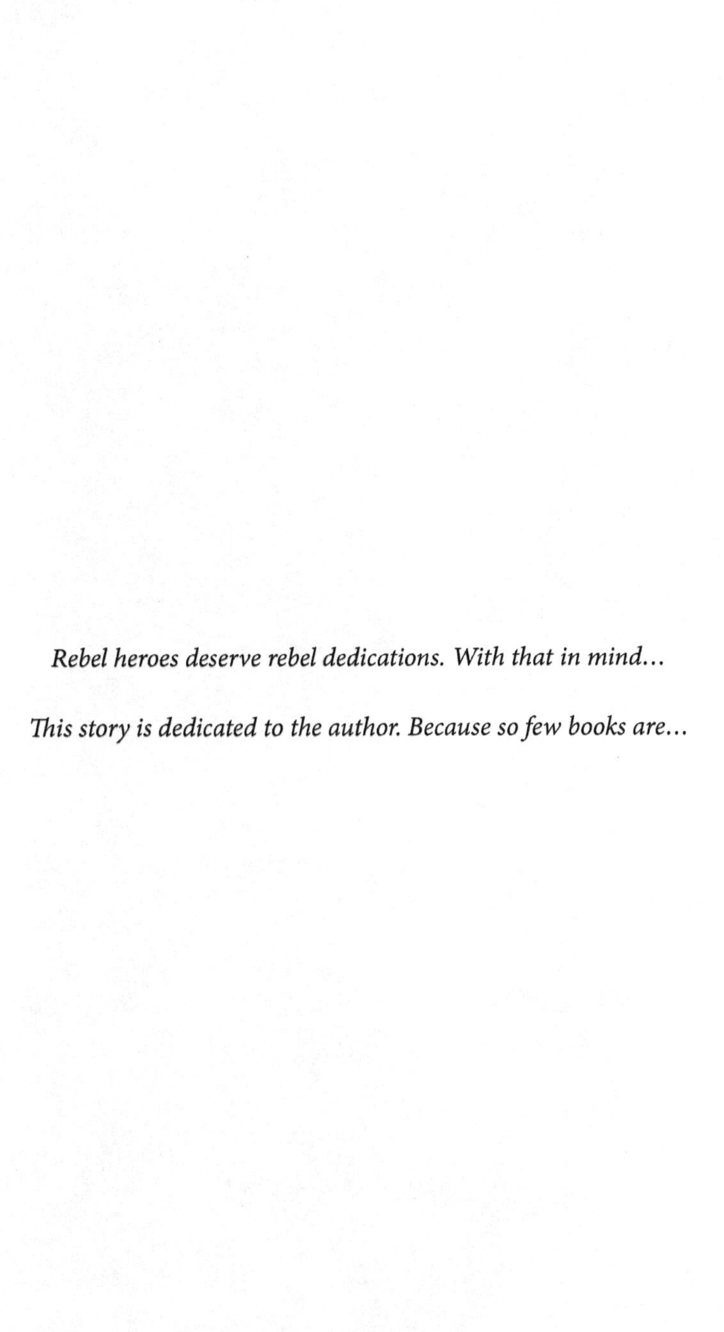

Rebel heroes deserve rebel dedications. With that in mind...

This story is dedicated to the author. Because so few books are...

CHAPTER 1

Oh my gods, did you see? Sebastian Collins is back again!"

Sebastian worked his boots off, trying not to grit his teeth. His jaw already ached enough as it was.

Another voice chimed in, *"I see him in the common room a few times a week. What's the big deal?"*

Second boot off. He aligned it with the first at the foot of the bed, rolled his shoulders, and winced. His bones were starting to feel tight. *Come on, what's the hold-up?*

"Girls draw straws to see who'll get to have him. He's so good, they do him for free, and Miss Kiki lets them!"

"You know why, though, right?"

Shouldn't walls in a brothel be thick enough to muffle sound? Sebastian crossed to the wash basin by the window and splashed cold water on his face.

"They say that years ago, he was a page in the castle. He was so beautiful, King Edgar's knights were jealous of him—and he was only sixteen!"

The basin rocked sharply in his grasp, splashing water onto the vanity.

"Even Queen Zorana lost her head when she saw him. After she offed

her husband, she tried to seduce him, but Sebastian blew her off. She got so mad she cursed him to feel increasingly more pain until it killed him unless he came back to please her. So he literally has to *make a girl come, as many times as she wants until she's satisfied."*

"But Zorana is dead. Didn't the curse die with her?"

"No one knows. Some say she used raw magic and it warped inside him. Others say it was flawed from the beginning because he never went back to her, but he's still alive."

The other girl scoffed. *"Faery tales."*

"No, it's true! I—"

A delicate knock on the door heralded his healer for the day. "Hello, lover."

Her voice immediately silenced the new girls next door, and Sebastian put them out of his mind at once. "Good morrow, Lacie."

She smiled softly. "You know, you're the only one who ever says that anymore? So old-fashioned." Today, her lips were painted a delicate pink, and her jet black hair was loose, trailing down her back in a smooth, straight fall. Minimal makeup to go with the soft, white silk dress that almost reached her knees. She'd gone for the innocent look, likely for one of her repeat customers. Sebastian didn't have a preference.

"I like to think it's classy. Shall we?"

"Let's."

Sebastian let her lie back on the bed, then shucked out of his leather tunic and undid the buttons on his shirt. His knuckles were starting to lock. Ignoring the pain and the creaking friction in his knees and hips, Sebastian knelt between Lacie's legs and inched the hem of her dress up her thighs. With a kiss to each of her knees, he slid his hands higher to hook his fingers into the waistline of her panties, drawing them down.

"So what are you in the mood for today?"

Lacie shrugged. "You know what I like."

Yeah, he did. For all of her popularity at Miss Kiki's as the blowjob queen of Kesteran, Lacie's preferences leaned more toward women than men. That was why Sebastian requested her as often as possible. A woman who liked his mouth on her was less likely to want his cock.

They had developed a sort of pleasant rhythm between them over the years. Sebastian knew what pleased Lacie, and in turn, she knew what to expect from him to the point where her body was almost trained to get wet for him as soon as she walked through the door. No complications, no exorbitant demands. Just a conversation between friends.

He could already feel Lacie's pulse racing where he held the back of her knee. Her nipples beaded against the silk of her dress, begging to be played with. Lacie herself did the honors, massaging her small breasts, pinching those nipples. She presented a picture straight out of a man's fantasies.

Sebastian remained completely unaffected. "Part your pretty thighs for me some more."

Lacie let her legs fall open, baring her sex to him. As most of the girls here, she was completely smooth, the lips of her sex already glistening. He kissed his way up the inside of her right thigh, licked the crease of her loin, then trailed open-mouthed kisses across her abdomen and back down the other side.

"Sebastian, please. Don't tease me today."

"Right you are, sweet." He didn't have time to play, anyway. Not if he wanted to make it to the castle on time for the Rebels' audience with Queen Snow. She so rarely called on them all at once, and the invitation was so vague, Sebastian half expected her to announce they were going to war again.

I'd welcome it.

"Hold on tight, sweet."

In answer, Lacie threaded her fingers through his hair, mewling his name. Sebastian set his mouth on her, licking sucking, nipping, until she writhed beneath him. He took his time to amp up her pleasure before he let her take it. Quick orgasms didn't do the trick. Better to work his partner up a little, or a lot, depending on how bad a state he was in.

Lacie's legs closed around him, she rocked her hips up to him, and he caught them firmly to keep her still as he flicked his tongue over her clit. When he felt her muscles clench, on the verge of coming, he eased off, let her come down a little before he set in again. He did it again, and again, until Lacie thrashed her head, begging him to let her come.

With one finger against her G-spot, he rubbed circles over her clit, breathing a covert sigh of relief as pleasure rocked her and the ache in his bones eased. But she wasn't finished yet, so neither was he. Keeping up a steady rhythm, he fucked her with his fingers, smoothly bringing her from one orgasm right into the next.

He didn't stop until she reached down with a shaky hand and pushed him away. "Gods, 'bastian. I feel like I should be paying you for that."

"I live to please," he answered with enough sarcasm to make it sound serious.

In her current, boneless state, Lacie took him at his word and smiled. "Shall I return the favor?" To her credit, she did make an attempt to reach for him, but like a drunk whose depth perception had been eroded hours ago, she ended up waving her hand in the air two feet in front of him.

Sebastian checked his watch. *Shit!* "Love to, sweet. Some other time, though."

"*Anytime*, lover."

Sebastian washed up, shoved his feet into his boots, grabbed his tunic, and went out the door, ignoring the dreamy looks and sighs the new girls gave him as he brushed past them. He jogged down the stairway, across the common room and out to the parking lot. The driver's side door of his sleek, black sports car opened with the push of a button and he ducked in easily, gunning the engine before the automatic door had even closed all the way.

With two minutes to spare, he pulled into the castle's courtyard and jumped out, engine still running for the valet to take over. He arrived at the boardroom in time for the grandfather clock to toll the hour and for Snow's ancient herald to appear and intone, "Her Majesty thanks you for your audience." All of Snow White's Rebel Court was in attendance, all of them standing to attention, ready to follow the herald inside, but he stayed them. "One at a time, if you please. Her Majesty will see Master Haig first."

Sebastian raised an eyebrow at that. What the hell was going on? His comrades seemed to be thinking the same, looking at each other in question, except Haig, who apparently thought this was hilarious. "I'll try not to wear her out too much." *Only Haig…*

When the door closed once more, the rest of them resumed their seats to wait for their turns.

"You cut it close," Declan told Sebastian in an aside.

"Couldn't be helped." Though he'd have appreciated Snow giving them a copy of whatever schedule she was working with so the rest of them didn't need to waste time waiting.

"Any change?" As their healer, Declan Rave didn't acknowledge the term "lost cause" as part of his vast vocabulary of medical definitions.

"Nope," Sebastian answered, the same way he always did. Even with Declan's…unconventional way of manipulating magic, he'd been unable to do shit about Sebastian's curse, so why he would expect the damned thing to change on its own, Sebastian didn't know. "Any new leads?"

Declan shook his head. "I keep searching, but nothing has come up yet." Which was healer-talk for "I have thirty possible theories to explore, but can't test any of them without potentially killing the subject so I won't even mention them." Declan still had hope for a cure. Sebastian had lost his a long time ago.

They fell into an uneasy silence after that, unbroken even by Beau's summons into the boardroom. Neither he nor Haig had yet come back out, which didn't bode well. He'd love to know what their lovely queen was up to.

Several minutes later, the door opened once more, and the herald called Sebastian by name. Sebastian stood, adjusting his white uniform. He'd left the top two buttons of his shirt undone; he doubted Snow would notice or care.

"Whatever this is about," Declan said, halting Sebastian in his tracks, "Be wary. I sense deep turmoil in our queen."

Frowning, Sebastian nodded and followed the herald into the boardroom. This was where Snow kept an eye on the welfare of Valefort. Today, the queen's brow furrowed unhappily as she watched the financial market lines dip and rise in real time on the monitors.

Beau had left his mark in the form of a stack of files and reports. It was a sign of Snow's deep respect for her master strategist that she'd left them on the table instead of shoving them all off into the trash bin as Sebastian would have done. Gods love that nerd, but he needed to cut down on his paper consumption.

"My queen looks troubled."

Snow White tore her gaze away from the monitors to face him. As always, an unspoken salute passed between them, an acknowledgment of their past, and the secrets they carried for each other. "Thank you for coming."

Sebastian bowed in answer. "Always a pleasure to see you. Shall we sit?"

She made no move to resume her seat. "Do you trust me, Sebastian?"

"Of course," he answered without hesitation.

"Do you trust me with your life?"

Sebastian tilted his head, but answered truthfully, "Yes."

Some of the tension left her shoulders, but her frown deepened. "I don't have official crown business to send you on," she said after a pause. "But yours might be the most dangerous mission of all. Are you prepared to obey, no matter the risk to yourself?"

"Just tell me what you want me to do." Snow had earned the unquestioning loyalty of every one of her Rebel Court many times over, but none owed her a greater debt than Sebastian. If she asked him to jump off the top of the bell tower, he'd do it gladly.

"I want you to heal," Snow replied.

Sebastian almost laughed. "I would if I could."

Snow crossed to the side cabinet and opened it onto an impressive stash of hard liquor. Lifting the edge of the tray, she slipped her hand underneath and withdrew a plain white envelope. She held it with both hands for a moment, as if waging some internal battle, then came back and handed it to him.

The name on it read Willow Faithblade. "Anyone I know?"

"Marcus' very distant cousin, on his mother's side."

Sebastian raised an eyebrow. "You're sending me to Sturmgard?"

Snow shook her head. "No, she's in Valefort. From what I was able to find out, Willow is the last living female descendant of Alvina Ericksson, Marcus' five times great aunt."

"Then she will be the last living Ericksson to carry their gift." Marcus' family possessed a unique immunity to the side effects of raw magic. All magic came at a price, and the more one used, the greater the risk of it going very wrong, but the Ericksson line was somehow able to draw on and manipulate raw magic without being adversely affected by it. The gift was genetically passed down from mother to daughter, and dictated their right to rule Sturmgard.

Sometimes, as in Marcus' case, a quirk of fate or love allowed a son the use of this gift as an extension of his mother's, but only for as long as she lived. When Marcus' mother, Ianna, had died, her magic had, as well.

The problem was, the Ericksson line had run out of female descendants with Ianna and, when attempt after attempt to replicate their ability artificially had failed, the burden of finding a different solution had fallen onto Marcus. That solution had been a merger with Valefort and the start of a thriving magic refinery business.

"But wait, if she's a legitimate heir, why wasn't she put forth to take over for Ianna?"

"Because she's only legitimate genetically," Snow replied. "The magic follows the blood, but the crown doesn't. Alvina was disinherited and banished from Sturmgard forever. Funny thing is, we know she and all of her future descendants were shunned by her family, but we don't know why."

"Must have been bad for them to resort to such drastic measures."

"That's what I'm thinking. In the entire history of the Ericksson royal line, there is no other record of a banishment before Alvina or since."

"And we found out about all this how?"

"Divine intervention," Snow retorted. "When Marcus turned down Zorana's offer of marriage, she set her bloodhounds on the trail of anyone else she could use instead. They were the ones who tracked down Willow but, by then, Zorana was already beaten."

Which meant Zorana hadn't had time to sink her claws into the woman and corrupt her. And that meant this Willow Faithblade now presented a real chance of lifting Zorana's curse from Sebastian.

He tried and failed to contain the spark of hope flaring into life inside him. *It won't work,* he told himself, even as his palm started to sweat, holding the envelope. *It never does.*

As if she sensed his growing excitement, Snow said, "There's a catch."

Sebastian couldn't prevent a sneer. "Of course there is."

"After so many years, we have no way of knowing whether Willow is even aware of her heritage, let alone how to use it."

"One way to find out."

She winced. "Yeah, that's the other catch. Open the envelope."

He did. It contained one piece of paper with a set of coordinates. "I'm not gonna like this, am I?"

The queen of Valefort shook her head. "We tracked her down in the White Plains. The good townsfolk of Icerton refer to her as 'that ghoul in the castle,' which we assume is the Helegert keep."

"You mean the Helegert *ruin.*" This just got better and better. "So I fly out there—"

"You can't fly. Or drive."

"What? Why the hell not?"

"Because there are no air fields up there, and only a handful of gas stations. The White Plains storms routinely wipe out entire roadways and disrupt any kind of transmissions, and this year they seem to be worse than ever. You can probably drive up as far as Oberland, but you'll need a horse and carriage the rest of the way."

Sebastian gaped at her. "I'm supposed to *ride* through the White Plains?"

Snow dropped her gaze for a moment, then looked back at him, her expression grave and serious. "This could very well be the last chance we'll have of ever setting you to rights again."

I know that! "It could also be a very quick and painful way to kill me."

"Yes." Well, at least she didn't try to lie. "I sent word ahead to prepare Willow for your arrival. She received all known details of your condition and past treatment attempts, so hopefully, she's already working on it, and you won't have to spend too much time there."

Well, fan-fucking-tastic. "Does Marcus know about this?"

"Of course he knows. I'm not going to go behind his back to contact the black sheep of his family without his permission."

"And he's on board?"

"We both agree that the risk is worth the potential benefit to you. Also, Marcus is hoping you can persuade Willow to 'migrate south' to meet him. He'd go to her himself but, without knowing the details of Alvina's banishment, he's afraid Willow will see his visit as an act of aggression. She is the only member of Ianna's family he has left now."

Then Marcus' request was a much bigger deal than Snow implied. "I thought you said this wasn't official crown business."

"It isn't. It's a request for a favor. And only if and after Willow can fix you."

Right. Because if she couldn't, Sebastian wouldn't live long enough to complete that favor.

But what if…?

CHAPTER 2

Willow frowned. "But I don't understand. You didn't have a problem with me creating a summer garden five years ago. Why is it a problem now?"

The ice fey chieftain narrowed his eyes, and a hissing sound emanated from him. Ice fey didn't speak, in the strictest sense of the word, but they still made themselves understood by some quirk of magic Willow had yet to uncover. Her study into that particular subject was being sabotaged by the ice fey's stubborn refusal to cooperate.

"Sprightlings? *That's* the problem?" She glanced over at the little foot-and-a-half tall creatures currently hiding behind a large maple tree. They looked like green children with oversized heads and big, insect-like eyes, and their presence alone did wonders for her garden's yield. "But they're so cute."

The ice fey's long, frozen hair rattled in irritation, and a glassy sheen of ice covered his clenched fist, a precursor to a frost grenade.

"Now, calm down. There's no need for violence. I can make sure they stay in my garden and don't damage yours." To be honest, she hadn't considered that the sprightlings would want to venture outside the confines of her summer garden. But it seemed the little rascals had a wily side.

"I can set up a boundary they won't be able to cross."

That set off more rattling.

"Well then what do you want?" She stomped her foot. "If you won't let me pen them in, then *you* do something. Ward your own gardens and that'll be that."

The ice fey bared his fangs—another mystery she itched to get to the bottom of—teeth made of ice.

Willow sighed. "The timing of your people's arrival in these lands was proven by earth records and magic sediment readings to post-date humans by two thousand years. We're not the interlopers, you are. If you don't like sprightlings melting your iced flower beds, by all means, move back to your own iceplane where no other living thing will bother you, including flowers."

If she had a door to slam in his face, she would have. Instead, she turned her back on him and returned to her harvest. Of all the nerve. Blaming *her* for the actions of a dozen little earth creatures causing mischief fifty miles up north. Ridiculous!

"You see the trouble you got me into?" she told the one gazing up at her from behind the maple.

In answer, it blinked its overlarge eyes and held out its tiny hand. In its palm was a shiny little crystal. A sapphire, probably, or a diamond. These lands were supposed to be peppered with them, but the ground was frozen most of the year, and the few weeks it thawed, the locals were usually too busy eking out a dismal harvest to look for riches.

Willow huffed and accepted the peace offering. "Leave the ice fey alone now. You have plenty of flowers to play with here." To say the least. Willow had thawed a full acre of the lands surrounding her home as an experiment to make herself a proper garden. She must have done something right, because that one acre had yielded beautiful fruits, vegetables, and flowers for five years now, and the harvests had only gotten larger with the sprightlings around.

Yet she still couldn't win favor with either of her neighbors. The ice fey to the north hated any magic that disrupted the White Plains with color, and the townspeople of Icerton were too jealous of her success to see how it could benefit them, too. Willow alone couldn't eat all of this, after all. She'd planned to share—for free! They'd spat in her face for her offer.

Sometimes it seemed like the sprightlings were the only ones who truly liked her. But, of course, they were only using her for her garden.

With a basket full of vegetables for her stew, Willow retrieved her thick coat, wrapped it tightly around herself, and headed back toward the keep. As soon as she passed the garden's stone archway, a frigid gust of wind snatched at her. The storm was getting worse. It'd be another cold night for Helegert. Good thing Willow was handy with raw magic, otherwise she'd have frozen to death long ago. A shame the stone couldn't hold heat as well as soft earth. No matter how hard she tried, Helegert's walls simply refused to stay warm.

In the kitchen, the stew base was coming along nicely over a sturdy flame. The hunk of smoked deer shank would give it flavor and much-needed protein. It'd need another hour or two to soften before she added the vegetables, then about thirty minutes to cook those down, and lunch would be ready.

She checked the clock. Well, maybe dinner. *Note to self: begin cooking lunch earlier in the day—*

A loud series of bangs echoed throughout the keep.

"What was that?"

The echoes had barely faded when three more bangs rang out, making her jump.

Had the ice fey come back?

Taking the cobweb-covered broom out of the corner as a makeshift weapon, Willow followed the sound out into the hallway to the ruined part of the keep. The banging had come from the massive front door.

"*Hello!*" someone shouted from the other side. She could see the edge of a furry winter hat through the hole in the wall by the door. But… Willow never got visitors. "*Hello!*" the irate stranger yelled again.

"Hello?" she called back softly.

"*Anyone in there?*"

Curious. Willow set the broom aside and went up to the hole in the wall. "Who's asking?"

The man sought her out in the dying light. "I'm looking for the mistress of this…castle."

"Is she expecting you?" *Am I?*

"She should be," he retorted, hopping in place and breathing on his hands to warm them. "The queen herself sent a message to notify her of my arrival."

"Oh. No, you're mistaken, sir. That's not for another week."

"Believe me, it isn't."

"No, no. I'm quite certain it's not until June the seventh."

"It's the eighth of June," he growled back.

"Since when!"

"Since sunrise! Will you just open the damn door already? I'm freezing out here."

Well, of course he was. The main door faced right into the storm streams that blew across the Plains every other month. Why would he stand out there in the first place? "You'll need to go around back. This door has been frozen shut since before I can remember."

Ambling back toward the kitchen, Willow counted the days. *Sunday, Monday, Tuesday…* Could she really have lost a week? The package from "Queen Snow of the House of White" still sat on the side table in the kitchen. When did Valefort get a new queen? And what happened to King Edgar?

Must have been a recent thing. Surely, the townspeople would have told her if something that monumental had happened. News didn't travel well this far north, but one would think a regime change would have been announced to all and sundry.

The stranger barged in through the kitchen door, no longer bothering to knock, and crossed straight to the fire to warm himself.

She had a visitor! The queen of House White had sent her a broken house guest for Willow to fix—how exciting! "Welcome to Helegert keep, sir. We are ever so pleased to have you." She dipped a quick curtsy, not caring that his back was still to her. Really, how often did she get to stand on ceremony?

Which reminds me, there's something I'm forgetting…

"Fetch your mistress," he said, shedding his thick coat and hat. "And my horses and carriage will need seeing to. I couldn't find your stables." He had a broad back that tapered to a narrow waist. His many layers obscured most of his physique, but it was still quite pleasing to the eye, even hunched as he was.

Caught up in the way the firelight played over his dark blond hair, Willow lost the thread of conversation. "Oh. Um, that's because we don't have stables. They were destroyed in the Battle of White Plains. Along with half of the keep. And, uh…I am the mistress. And also the only one in residence here. Lady Willow Faithblade, at your service, mister…?"

Finally, he turned to face her. As handsome from the front as he was from the back, with thick eyebrows lowered in a scowl and dark circles beneath eyes the color of shimmering blue-green northern lights.

Willow nearly sighed.

An angel. Even the sickly pallor of his skin and his hollowed cheeks couldn't mar the sensual bow of his mouth or the proud jut of his chin. How utterly unfair that his flaws didn't diminish his looks in the least, but enhanced them with a human fragility and sorrow that softened the cold perfection of his features.

His scowl gave way to a blank expression of surprise. "What happened to your hair?"

Shaken out of her wandering thoughts, Willow frowned. "My hair?" Willow adjusted her spectacles on her nose, then reached up to pat her hair. It felt the same as always. She took a section of it in hand and held it up to the light. It looked the same as always, too.

"It's gray."

"Yes." What else could she say to that?

He kept staring.

Maybe she ought to give him some time to recover. After the long trip from Kesteran to the White Plains, he had to be exhausted. Unsure of what else to say, Willow decided the simplest solution would be for her to go away. So she did.

"Wait—*wait!*" The handsome stranger caught up to her in the hallway and barred her path, taking a step back when she didn't stop in time. He carried the scent of snow on his skin, but beneath it, Willow caught a hint of him. "I'm sorry; I didn't mean to offend you. I just didn't expect… Your hair is lovely."

He smelled of summer. Warmth, vitality, sunshine, and sex—

What in the world? "I don't have a guest room," Willow blurted out, fighting hard to suppress the damning flush that crept up her cheeks. "I forgot. There's only the one room still intact and the kitchen. I was going to send word back to the Queen of House White, but then the ice fey showed up, and I got distracted." *I do that a lot,* she wanted to add but bit her tongue. What must he already think of her, to have forgotten he was coming in the first place?

"I see," he said, still staring at her hair, but making a visible effort not to, which only made her more conscious of his staring. "Let's start over. My name is Sebastian Collins. I was sent by Queen Snow to petition your aid in a personal matter. I assume you know what I'm referring to?"

"Oh, yes, the package was quite informative. Fascinating curse. I can't wait to learn more about it."

The polite mask he'd put on fractured into something brittle, small, and tired. "You mean you haven't found a cure yet?"

"How could I have found a cure without the curse? What a silly notion."

Willow could feel his frustration well up like an approaching avalanche that made her ears pop. Had she said something wrong? "You do realize time is of the essence," he grated.

"Naturally. Would you like to begin now?"

He smiled, but it looked forced. "Please."

"Very good. You can lead your horses and carriage to the summer garden. It's just past the tree line. They'll be warm there, and have plenty of food. I'll finish the stew in the meantime, and we can reconvene over dinner."

He nodded. "That'll work."

I'm going to die, Sebastian thought as he drove the horses against the winds to the "summer garden" behind the ruin's kitchen. *I'm going to die in the frozen fucking north, in a cave of a ruin, owned by an owl with gray hair and ashtray spectacles.*

Past the tree line, a stone wall cut across the land, but through the archway opening, he saw an impossible sight. Northern winds blustered all around him, the ground was frozen solid beneath his feet, and snow and ice covered everything as far as the eye could see, but inside that stone fence, the sun shone down on green grass and bright flowers. Not a single leaf swaying in the breeze.

Sebastian shook himself. The archway wasn't wide enough to drive through, so he unhitched his matched pair and led them through one after the other. Summer garden was a fitting name for what was literally a different season carved into a patch of the White Plains.

She couldn't have done that around the castle?

How could she live in that place? *Why* would she choose to live there, instead of building up a cozy little cottage out here?

With the horses settled, he braced himself for another battle with the elements to fetch his bag out of the carriage and return to the kitchen. What the hell could Alvina have done that was so bad it got her sent out here in punishment?

Inside the kitchen, the fire burned hot, but it still wasn't enough to warm the cavernous chamber sufficiently. The dilapidated wooden table was set with two bowls and spoons, and Willow was at the cauldron, stirring her stew. In his absence, she'd braided her wild hair neatly back.

Because of him? That didn't sit right.

"With you in a moment," she said, then took a sip of broth from the wooden spoon. Her gown moved up and down her sides as she raised and lowered her arms, clearly sewn for someone shorter and much wider, and for a split second, the baffling impulse popped into Sebastian's head to wonder what she'd look like beneath all that wool.

He shook himself and flexed his hands to work some warmth into his half-frozen fingers. "Anything I can do to help?"

She added more seasonings to the stew and pointed back without looking away from the pot. "There are goblets in the top cabinet there. And I think there's still a bottle of wine in bottom one."

Sebastian brushed back the cobwebs and retrieved two dust-filled goblets. Nothing else on those shelves, except an empty liquor decanter and a pile of crystals. The bottom cabinet door fell off its rusted hinges when he opened it. He shook his head and set it aside. "No wine in here," he announced. At least none that he could see, and he wasn't about to stick his hand into that black, likely vermin-filled hole.

Willow licked her fingers with a *smack*, then came over and nudged him aside to kneel in front of the cabinet. Her entire top half disappeared into it, defying all laws of physics he knew, and moments later, a triumphant, "Aha!" echoed in there. She shimmied her butt as she reemerged, with an ancient-looking bottle in hand and a thick cobweb hanging from the rim of her glasses. "I knew I still had one left."

"You don't get much company up here, do you?"

She looked up at him through those ridiculously thick glasses that made her eyes look enormous. "How did you know?"

Sebastian caught the cobweb and pulled it off her glasses. "Lucky hunch."

"This place used to be a tourist attraction back in the day. People would come from all over to carve ice sculptures and watch the northern lights. But when the main keep was destroyed, they stopped coming."

"Why did you stay?" he asked as he helped her to her feet. The old-fashioned woolen dress had to weigh at least a ton. Layered over a thick sweater, the bodice was still loose, the faded sleeves didn't quite reach her wrists, and the skirt just brushed her ankles.

Willow shrugged. "This is my home. Where else would I go?"

Beneath the wild gray hair and crazy specs, she was actually very pretty, and despite the distance of their relations, she looked a great deal like Valefort's handsome king. The same nose, the same stubborn chin, but her features were more delicate, her lips fuller, and her eyes a darker shade of brown. The harsh weather had lent her a waiflike leanness. She was pale, but her cheeks and lips were bright red. She looked like an abandoned porcelain doll, and Sebastian found it strangely appealing.

A true connoisseur would take his time with a morsel like Willow. He'd savor stripping down the worn rags piece by piece, wiping away the cobwebs and brushing through her hair to reveal the beauty hidden beneath years of neglect. And she would shine so bright…

Willow held up the bottle. "Shall we eat?" she asked.

The cold had to be getting to him. Sebastian nodded and followed her directions to rinse the goblets in the water barrel by the fireplace. Then helped her open the wine and poured for both of them while she ladled stew into the bowls. "It's not much, but it'll fill you up."

"I'm sure it's great," he said to be polite, but the stew turned out to be quite tasty and rich. They ate in silence, sipped wine that had aged much stronger than the usual Kesteran vintage. Sebastian didn't mind. At this point, anything that raised his body temperature was a welcome boon.

And all the while he watched the strange creature sitting across from him, almost imperceptibly bouncing in her seat while staring into the depths of her bowl, and he couldn't look away.

When they finished, Sebastian sat back and watched impatiently as Willow cleaned their dishes. "About my curse," he said when she finished and reached for the broom.

"Ah, yes." She came back to the table, adjusted her glasses and leaned in almost nose-to-nose with him, staring into his eyes. "The queen's letter said this happened about fourteen years ago?"

A skein of her hair slipped free of her braid, sliding closer and closer toward his face. His entire body went taught, joints groaning in protest, bones twisting almost to the breaking point. "That's right," he answered thickly. Her mouth looked like it had been painted on by a master artist, lush and soft, and cherry red, begging to be kissed and, though he was in too much physical discomfort to get hard, Sebastian suddenly wished he could.

He wanted to take that ridiculous dress off her and spread her on the table like a banquet for his feast. He wanted to lick the wine off her pale skin and make it heat to his touch. He wanted her sighs in his ear and her hands on him—anywhere. Everywhere.

I'm finally losing my mind.

Sebastian had always known it would happen sooner or later. No one could endure this kind of pain and stay sane for long. Fourteen years. Gods, it was a miracle he'd lasted this long.

But why now? Why her?

"And do you remember where you were struck?"

He frowned, tearing his gaze away from her lips to focus on her eyes. "Pardon?"

Her spectacles slipped lower on her nose, and she reached up to adjust them, shading the fire's light for long enough to deepen the intimacy to an unbearable degree. "A curse is like an arrow," she lectured, oblivious to the effect she had on him. "You would have been shot somewhere specific, like an arm or the head. It's likely that when it activates, it does so from that particular location."

Invisible spear stabbing through his heart. Agony so intense it stole his breath away and sent him to his knees, but he had to keep going, keep moving forward. To stop now meant capture, and a fate worse than death…

"The chest." He cleared his throat to regain his voice. "I was struck in the chest."

"Remove your sweater and shirt, please." She stood up straight to allow him to undress.

Sebastian's fingers were going numb with the cold. He stripped down to the waist, moving closer to the fire.

Willow came up to him again, staring hard at the center of his chest. She raised her hands as if to touch him, but didn't make physical contact. Instead, her palms hovered a fraction of an inch from his skin, and Sebastian felt something akin to static electricity. "I can see it," she said, her warm breath puffing against him, agitating his already frayed nerves. No one had ever examined him with such deep scrutiny before, except Declan. "It's like a starburst right here…" A cool fingertip touched the dead center of his chest. "Does it hurt now?"

"No," he answered automatically, his entire being focused on that small point of contact as she took it back.

"You're lying to me."

Sebastian winced. "Force of habit, I'm afraid." The truth was, the pain never went away completely, it only varied in intensity. But people didn't want to know that. It made for awkward silences and pitying looks he'd just as soon not deal with, so pretending everything was fine had become second nature to him over the years. Only Snow and the other Rebels knew the whole truth, and they knew better than to ask.

Willow sighed and straightened away from him. "If I'm to help you, I must have the truth."

She kept talking, but Sebastian couldn't concentrate on her words. That static of her nearness was fading fast, and he felt its loss down to his bones. A completely insane thought popped into his head to snatch her against him and kiss that lush mouth, tug her hair free so he could wind it around his hand—

"Are you listening?"

"Yes," he lied. "Truth only. Understood."

She stalled for a suspicious moment before coming back to him to continue her examination. Her hair smelled like ice and smoke, but underneath that, he caught the subtlest hint of her own, natural scent, and it made him want to bury his nose in her gray mane and breathe in deep to get more of it. He swayed, light headed as she circled him, cocooning him in her presence, and that damned static sank deep into him wherever she almost touched, never fully connecting.

"What does it feel like?"

"What?" He wanted her hands on him so bad it hurt almost as much as the curse. What was he thinking? It *was* the curse. It had to be.

She cast him an uncertain glance. "The pain. Is it dull? Sharp? Do you feel it in your stomach, your muscles…?"

Sebastian cleared the hoarseness out of his throat. "It's a constant ache deep in my bones," he admitted. "If the curse isn't satisfied, my spine and joints lock up, and I lose fine motor function."

Willow took his hand in hers, examined his knuckles with the same scrutiny she'd shown his chest. Her touch was so light he barely felt it, yet it still raised gooseflesh up his arm.

He swallowed hard. "As it gets worse, it feels like all my bones have been crushed into shards with the edges scraping against each other."

She trailed her fingers up his forearm to the elbow, then up to the shoulder and, without thinking, Sebastian flexed his bicep. Shocked at himself, he forced his mind back to what he was saying "After that, it spreads to my torso and skull."

The worst it'd ever been, Sebastian had been rendered immobile, his jaw locked and his ribs screeching with every breath he'd drawn, no matter how shallow. He'd been unable to even scream as thousands of sharp bone fragments had seemed to stab into his brain.

"I see," she said, her almost-touch trailing across his collarbone, then over to his shoulder blade. He felt that static against the center of his spine, flowing down to his lower back. The flat of her palm never connected with him entirely, and it frustrated the hell out of him. "And sex is the only thing that satisfies it?"

"Sex alone doesn't cut it. My partner's pleasure is required. Zorana was very specific when she cast her curse."

"What precisely did she say?"

"Her handmaid confessed after Zorana's death that the spell she cast was in tongues. An ancient book of incantations was found in Zorana's private chambers, and we managed to piece together the most likely combination to have yielded this result."

She probed his hip through his pants. "You didn't hear it yourself?"

Sebastian shook his head. "No one except the handmaid did, and she was too terrified to recall more than a fraction of what she'd heard."

"Hmm."

What did that mean? What was she doing back there? "Based on everything we know, the most plausible theory is that her use of raw magic corrupted her spell and removed it from her control. It allowed me to mitigate the effects with other women, and the curse to survive her death." He craned his head to look over his shoulder, but her head was bent as she stared at his spine. "All of this should have been in Snow's report."

"Oh, it was."

"Then why all the questions?"

"Because it doesn't make sense." She huffed and came back around to face him. Hands on her hips, she glared at his stomach. And it decided to flex. Because why the fuck not? "One last question. Can you have sex for its own sake?"

He almost laughed. "The better question would be: Do I want to?"

That inquisitive owlish gaze raised up to clash with his once more. "Do you?"

I must have the truth, she'd told him.

"No," he answered honestly.

So why did it taste like a bitter lie?

CHAPTER 3

O h." Well, that was disappointing. What a waste of such a superb specimen. But Willow supposed it was only to be expected, given the circumstances. It didn't make her any less sorry for it. He was the kind of man women dreamed about taking to their beds. Less than an hour in his company and Willow herself started feeling overheated in her gown. What would it feel like to have that vast expanse of warm skin pressed against hers, to have his hands trace her body, and his mouth kissing the breath out of hers?

Her eyelids turned heavy as she answered herself: It'd be glorious.

"So, can you remove it?"

An unholy amalgamation of raw magic, three soul spells and four blood curses that had survived its caster's death? "I can try."

The starburst on his chest would be invisible to the naked eye, because it wasn't *on* him, precisely. It was *within* him, shining out of him, with all its jagged, spiky edges. Not surprising that it caused such excruciating pain.

Willow rubbed her hands together until her palms warmed. It awakened her senses, and she began to feel pockets of raw magic humming all around her, pulling on her like magnets. A hint of it lit up that cursed starburst even brighter.

"Hold still," she warned, then placed her hands on his chest, making a triangle with her thumbs and forefingers around the curse's mark. Sebastian hissed in a breath, pushing back against her palms, increasing contact beyond what she'd planned, and her hands…stuck.

Biting heat licked along her skin as she felt the curse respond to her closeness, and its spikes lengthened, stabbing farther into Sebastian. "Do you feel any different?" she asked, keeping her voice calm while her heartbeat sped up with a stab of fear. What if she made it worse?

"No," he said.

"Are you lying to me?" She couldn't look up at him to check.

Sebastian chuckled. "A little."

"Tell me what you're feeling."

Another sharp inhale. "Heat. Like firebrands." His flesh was warming beneath her touch, yet he never moved, even though, feeling a small part of his torment, Willow knew his body was already wracked with terrible pain.

Willow focused her will on the raw magic inside him and pulled on it. "And now?" A thin strand seeped out, seeking her as its new seeding ground. She refused it entrance, forcing it instead to dissipate in the air, drop by tiny drop.

"It's cooling."

"Good. That's very good. Keep talking." She increased the draw, pulling out another strand, and then a third. As it leeched out of him, the starburst spikes shortened, retreating into the main tangle. The points dulled, curled inward until it resembled a tight ball of yarn.

"I can breathe easier. The ache is lessening. My joints feel looser. Holy shit, it's working!"

His excitement sent his heart racing, which agitated the ball to pull tighter, fighting her pull. Willow fought back, but the seep of raw magic slowed, then stopped, withdrawing back into him.

"You did it, didn't you?" he said, looking ten years younger from a moment ago.

Willow hung her head. "No." She *felt* his hope die and dropped her hands to her sides. "Not yet, anyway. I weakened it, I think, but it's still there."

He took her left hand in both of his and pressed it back to his chest.

"Then try again."

The warmth of his flesh coursed up her arm and sent shivers down her spine. How long had it been since another person had touched her? Willow wanted more of that warmth and shrank away from the foreignness of the physical sensation at the same time. "Not yet."

"Why the hell not?" Willow flinched at his shout, and he winced. "I'm sorry. I didn't mean to shout. I just don't understand."

He was even warmer than she'd imagined. Now that some of his pain was relieved, he vibrated with a vitality Willow wanted to soak into every inch of herself. She wanted to rub herself all over him like a cat until her hair grew electrified with the static she could feel humming beneath the surface of his skin.

He was the most amazing thing she had ever felt. So much life. So much passion and feeling, all trapped inside a prison of pain…

Of course he wanted to be free of it. Standing this close, Willow felt how desperate he was for her to keep going. She struggled to collect her words into a proper sentence. "You were a warrior, yes?"

Sebastian nodded.

He still held her hand to his chest. Should she remind him? If she did, he'd let go. "Well, to put it in familiar terms, my surprise attack was successful in weakening the enemy line, but reinforcements arrived faster than I anticipated."

"So what happens now?"

So warm. So alive… "We wait it out," she said, hardly hearing herself. "Find its weaknesses." His skin was tanned golden, almost the shade of a doe's hide and all she could think of was sunshine and summer, and lying naked in the grass, basking in it all. With him. "Destroy it from within…"

"Willow?"

"Yes?"

He freed a hand to tip her face up, and she finally looked away from his chest and met his gaze. Her face heated with embarrassment to have been caught staring like a loon. "I'm sorry. What were we talking about?"

The little relief she'd been able to provide by momentarily weakening the curse's power had banished the circles under his eyes, rendering him even more beautiful. A golden angel fallen from the sky, straight into her dilapidated home.

And he wasn't turning away from her. In fact, his gaze was so steady, so intense, it was almost as if he wanted to kiss her. Oh, if only that were true. Willow would give anything to taste that glorious sunshine from his lips. His face lowered toward her so slowly she stopped breathing in anticipation. *Just one taste. That's all.*

What happened to your hair?

"Sleeping arrangements," she blurted out.

He stopped, blinking those blue-green eyes at her. "What?"

She made her fingers uncurl from his belt—when did that happen?—and with more effort than should have been necessary, she stepped back and reclaimed her other hand from his clutch. "As I mentioned, there's only the one room fit for habitation at Helegert: mine. I don't mind sharing, but the bed is rather small. Won't fit two."

His mouth quirked in a quicksilver smile. "How do you suggest we solve this dilemma?"

"Well… Umm…"

Sebastian chuckled. "Rest easy. I got a file on you, too. I came prepared." He shrugged his shirt and sweater back on, then retrieved the large bag he'd dropped beside the door earlier.

Willow frowned. "You got a file on *me*? What was in it?"

"All right, *file* may be a bit of an exaggeration. It was more of a two-page report."

"Ah. Yes, that would make more sense." Willow wasn't exactly file-worthy. Most people forgot she even existed up here until she reminded them with one of her rare visits into town.

She waved toward the hallway, then led the way out of the kitchen toward her bedroom. *Leading a man to my bedroom.* A man she'd only just met, who had no interest in sex. Such a thing could only have happened to her.

Up the narrow, winding staircase she went, edging around the hole in the tower wall, and emerged into the second-floor hallway. With a snap of her fingers, she summoned a dozen tiny faery lights.

"This is the creepiest place I've ever been in," Sebastian said. He was so close Willow could feel his warmth against her back.

Tugging her braid forward, she toyed with the end, trying to imagine what her home must look like to him. To her, it was simply home. "I suppose castles down south are a bit more—"

"Habitable? Yes." He tripped over a boulder she'd stepped around, knocking into her. "Gods, how do you not kill yourself in this place on a daily basis? It's a death trap."

"I prefer to think of it as a strategic passive defense system," Willow replied peevishly. She was well aware that her home wasn't the most luxurious abode around, but it was still home, and it was hers, and she'd done quite well for herself in it.

Opening the wooden door she'd lovingly painted with colorful vines and knotwork, Willow waved Sebastian in ahead of her. "Originally, this was a suite of apartments that housed the master, mistress, and their personal servants," she explained. "Now the master chambers are buried under stone and rubble, and the foyers are missing the outer wall. Don't go through that door, there's nothing but a three-story drop on the other side."

Willow grew the faery lights so he could see better and watched him take in the layers of old tapestries hanging on the walls, the small bed she'd magically altered from a child's size to one that would fit her tall frame, and the two armoires, each propped up with a stone in one corner where a leg was missing.

He tapped his foot against the hard-packed dirt covering the floor, then raised a questioning look at her.

"Oh, this stone won't hold heat," she explained.

The look didn't go away.

"So…I need something softer," she added.

Still nothing.

"Because I can't build a fire in here."

Sebastian looked down, then back at her. "You use *dirt* to warm your bedroom?"

Willow shrugged. "It works."

"All right, then."

Across from her bed was a doorway barred with a massive fallen beam. "And that?" Sebastian asked, pointing at it.

"That's the bathing room. It's still accessible; you just have to duck under the beam."

"I shudder to think what might be on the other side."

Why? Why did he insist on being rude? "There's a hot spring half a mile to the east if you'd prefer that. Or perhaps the Icerton Inn might be more fit for your high standards."

"I'm sorry, I don't mean to be insulting, it's just… You have magic. Why not use it to make Helegert more comfortable for yourself?"

Willow blinked. "But I have." She'd repaired, insulated, cleaned, and restored whatever she could, but magic wasn't limitless.

And it wasn't as if she could hire a crew to come restore the place. Icerton was the only village around for miles and miles, and most of the time, Willow couldn't even get the people there to acknowledge her existence. They all labored under the mad notion that she was some kind of evil witch and Helegert was cursed. They sold her things she couldn't grow or make because she paid for them with gold coins, but that seemed to be the limit of their tolerance. They wouldn't come within miles of the keep itself and refused to take anything she tried to give them, even if they desperately needed it. Like the produce from her summer garden.

Sebastian looked dubious but didn't comment. "I suppose I can set up a mattress in this corner if that's all right with you."

Willow nodded, partly because it was the only option, and partly because he'd already begun to pull things out of his bag. One of them was a bundle with a pull cord he yanked out before tossing the thing on the floor. As Willow gaped, it hissed and expanded until a plump mattress lay there, twice as wide as her own bed. "That's new."

"The latest and greatest in air mattress technology. No blowing required." He spread a blanket over it, then rolled a thick jacket into a pillow. Should she tell him she had plenty of pillows he could use? No, he'd probably turn his nose up at them, anyway.

When he finished, he sat back on his heels and shook his head. "It's so weird. I should be exhausted and in agony after the trip up here. Instead, I feel like running circles around this ruin." He gave her a crooked smile. "Whatever healing magic you laid on me, it worked one hell of a miracle. I haven't felt this good since before the war."

The man had a smile that made her knees go weak.

Wait…

"Valefort went to war? With whom?"

He gaped. "With…itself?"

"When? And while we're on the subject, who's Queen Snow of House White, and what happened to King Edgar?"

Sebastian whistled. "Ho-ly shit. That's one hell of a story to tell."

Willow hopped onto her bed, tucked her feet under the bearskin throw, and waved him on. "I have time." She had nothing but time.

"Fair enough," he allowed, then sat on his mattress, with his back against the wall and his arms resting on his up-drawn knees. "What's the last you heard about the goings-on in Kesteran?"

Willow thought back to her lessons. "King Edgar got crowned after his parents stepped down. They died a few weeks later. People said it was a bad omen for his reign."

"Edgar married Lady Elspeth from the southern provinces. She was a great beauty, kind and gentle, and she made Edgar happy, but she died giving birth to his daughter, Snow. King Edgar was heartbroken. He raised Snow by himself for years, refused to entertain any thought of another wife, but eventually, the loneliness and the burden of ruling a kingdom on his own became too much. He married a titleless daughter of a lesser noble called Zorana Pomfrey…"

As he talked, Willow fiddled with her hands, weaving a subtle magic. Sebastian's voice grew softer, more monotone. His eyelids drooped as he yawned and slumped where he sat on his air mattress. In less than five minutes, wholly unaware of what'd happened, he was sound asleep.

Willow hopped off her bed. "Let's have a proper look at you, then." She grasped his long legs by the ankles and dragged them sideways to straighten him on the mattress. "Gods, you're a heavy one…" Winded by the time her task was complete, she took a moment to stretch out her back and catch her breath, then, fists to her hips, she surveyed her patient.

The curse still throbbed with sinister light within his chest. The tight yarn-like ball it had curled into was loose, relaxing as his body slumbered. As she watched, one tendril slipped free, seeming to fall out of the bundle, but then it stretched, twining in and out of his ribcage, seeking a new place to anchor. She may have *altered* the curse's makeup, but she hadn't weakened it by any means.

"Time to get to work."

Willow rubbed her hands together, drawing magic into her palms, then hiked up her skirts and straddled Sebastian's prone body. He breathed in deep a she settled astride him and Willow felt his member harden beneath the curve of her behind. Momentarily distracted, she stared down at his sleeping face, trying to read his subconscious thoughts. He'd said he didn't want sex, hadn't he? The constant pain would likely be a powerful deterrent, in any case.

But that had been his waking mind talking. What about when he slept? What would a man like Sebastian dream about? While his natural defenses were lowered in slumber, Willow theoretically had the skill to peek into his dreams, but two things stopped her: her respect for the man who had endured fourteen years of relentless physical torment and her fear of what she might see.

Willow already knew she wasn't the type of woman men fantasized about; she didn't need it irrefutably confirmed. Especially not while she was literally a few scant layers of cloth away from the most intimate contact a woman could make with a man.

Bringing her focus back to the task of curing him instead, she tugged Sebastian's shirt out of his waistband and pulled it up to expose his chest. One hand on either side of his sternum, fingers splayed to cover as much surface area as possible, she pressed down on his chest, weaving her magic with the curse to create a hook she could use to pull it out.

The trick was getting a firm enough hold to gain traction without sticking to it herself, and with a curse this complex, that was some trick, indeed.

Carefully maneuvering around the waking tendrils, Willow contained them one after the other and positioned herself for extraction.

Sebastian stirred beneath her, his hips curling up into hers, jarring her position. She gasped, stilled, barely containing her shiver before it lost her all the progress she'd made. *It's all right,* she assured herself. *Everything's fine, as long as he remains sleep—*

Sebastian's eyes opened.

CHAPTER 4

Dreaming. *Have to be.* Sebastian was prone on the mattress, his shirt undone, and an enchanting female with thick spectacles on her nose straddling him. He reacted without thinking, his lips curling into a sleepy smile as he reached out to tunnel his fingers into her thick, gray mane.

His upper body raised off the mattress to meet her halfway, and his mouth cut off whatever protest she tried to sputter with a kiss. He'd expected her lips to be warm, her cheeks heated with desire. Instead, the temptress' soft skin was cool as he cupped her jaw and throat.

Sebastian couldn't stop himself from tasting her if he'd tried. His tongue speared between her lips, savoring the taste of her surprised moan as he made love to her mouth. Like drinking out of an enchanted well. Snaking an arm around her slight hips he hugged her harder down on top of his cock, biting back a groan at the feel of her soft flesh against his hard length.

Too many layers between them. In some distant corner of his mind, he registered something out of sorts with that, but then she curled her little nails into his chest, and the thought dissipated. Sebastian's hand fisted in her hair. He tore his lips from hers, but only so he could taste more of her flesh; trail his tongue over her elegant throat; feel the flutter of her heartbeat there.

Her high collar impeded his progress. Another faint warning flag. The fire of his need burned it to ash in an instant. He heard her speaking breathy words, pleading, almost desperate. Rolling them both over, Sebastian pinned her beneath him, thrust against her as his clumsy fingers worked on the fastenings of her old-fashioned dress.

It'd been ages since he'd seen a laced bodice that didn't give with the slightest tug. More warnings. Didn't matter. Not when her lithe body arched up to him, her hands clawing at him to give her more. He could feel the tension in her; his curse telling him she was just as mired in her need as Sebastian. He worked that need into a fever pitch, digging his toes into the dirt floor to keep his own in check until he got her there.

She cried his name. Sebastian gave up on the laces, palmed her small breast through the thick layers of fabric. He could barely feel her, but she could feel him. Her hips moved with him, matching his rhythm in a primal dance that swept them both up in the moment.

Need more. He claimed her lips again, coaxed her tongue out to play, and reveled in the taste of her, the heady, mindless pleasure of enjoying a woman for no other reason than they both wanted to.

Apprehension skittered up his spine even as a weight seemed to lift from his chest. The woman beneath him tensed, arching as pleasure swept over her. She cried out, and he ate up the sound, taking it into his very soul. Gooseflesh made every square inch of his body so sensitive, he lasted one more thrust before he came, and came so hard he had to bury his roar against her shoulder.

Shuddering lightheaded, Sebastian held still, reeling from what'd just happened. When he perceived his partner squirming beneath him, he rolled to his side so she'd have room to breathe. Her hands, still on his chest, pulled away, and his flesh almost followed. Somehow, they'd become two magnets, inexplicably drawn together, and parting seemed impossible.

"Oh…" she breathed, her large eyes wide behind her spectacles.

Sebastian's brain re-engaged by degrees, slow and fuzzy, but he recognized her, and his surroundings. That apprehension he'd felt earlier burst into a full-on, "What the fuck!" that came out pathetically hoarse, more like a pleasure groan than an oath.

"Oh, my…"

"The hell did you do to me?" He pushed away, his entire being protesting the separation, and sat up, shaking his head. The buzzing between his ears grew louder, then softened and finally stopped and he could think.

Taking mental inventory, he found no pain in his bones. Remembering the healing she'd done on him after dinner, he forgot to breathe for a moment as he realized he'd just come. In his pants. With Willow.

Sebastian couldn't remember the last time he'd felt physical desire of any kind, let alone a true blue, stand-your-hair-on-end orgasm. Not since before the curse, probably.

And now this.

With Willow?

He didn't know whether to laugh or weep. "Does this mean I'm cured?" Sebastian could hardly believe it, but what the hell else was he supposed to think?

"Uh, not quite," Willow said. She looked kind of spooked.

"What does that mean?"

Willow sat up, adjusted her bodice, and tried to get her thoughts back into some semblance of order. Her body was still humming from the orgasm expertly delivered at the hands of what had to be the most masterful seducer in Valefort, and her mind was well and truly blown. If he could do that to her with all of their clothes still on, what in the world would it be like when they took them off?

"Willow?"

"Huh? Oh." He'd asked her what she'd meant. *What did I say again?* She frowned at his chest for a moment before her magical sight returned and showed her what she'd managed to accomplish. "Oh…" Oh, this was bad. Very, very bad.

"Stop saying 'oh.' I want to know why I woke up with you on top of me. Wait, when did I even fall asleep?"

"I, umm, the curse was too tricky to unravel while you were awake, so I thought it might go better if you were asleep."

That look of wary hope returned. "And?"

Willow pushed to her feet and turned away from him to straighten her bed. It was either that, or launch herself back at him and demand more of those dizzying kisses. "And I was correct. I had the curse well in hand before..."

"Before I woke up and broke your concentration," he finished. She heard him huff a sigh behind her. "All right, give it to me straight. How badly did I fuck this up for myself?" He may as well have been whispering lurid things right in her ear, the way her body responded to the mere sound of his voice.

Willow shook her head hard. "Not at all. Really. Just a minor delay, that's all. We tried a path and got part way to the finish line. Now we have to find another one to go the rest of the way."

"Is that why you won't look at me now?"

He'd come closer. She could sense him almost close enough to touch and had to brace herself when her knees weakened. Her cheeks flushed beet red. Good thing he couldn't see. She picked up a pillow to fluff and beat into the proper shape.

"Or did I freak you out?"

A down feather shot out of a corner seam and wafted through the air past her shoulder.

"I'm sorry. I don't know what came over me. I'm not usually so... Since the curse struck me, I haven't really..." Another huff. "I'll move down to the kitchen."

Willow whirled around. "You'll freeze to death!"

"Obviously I can't stay here."

"Why? Because we got a little carried away? Why do you even assume it was your fault? You were asleep, remember? Because I enchanted you. I could just as easily have been taking advantage of you."

They were toe-to-toe, and she could see a muscle twitch in his jaw. "Were you?" he asked, his voice low, dangerous. And still, the rumble of it made butterflies swarm in her belly.

Willow flushed. "I… I don't know." She couldn't be sure of anything while her chest still thrummed with the oddness of the tether that had sprung to life during their…indiscretion. A thin line of magic stretched between them, from his chest to hers, with the knot of his curse spinning over it, pulling it tighter. Pulling her mercilessly closer to him.

Willow swayed forward, hands curled into her skirts so she wouldn't reach out to touch him again, but his scent was intoxicating, the heat of his skin so inviting. Her breath hitched a little faster, a little shallower; her lips became so dry she had to lick moisture back into them.

Sebastian grasped her upper arms, his thumbs caressed her through the sleeves of her dress, and then he exerted just enough pressure to make her step back. "We should get some sleep."

Reading the words on his lips, Willow nodded. "Yes. Sleep. You should definitely do that." She walked out of the room with barely a thought to where she was going, her body moving by memory and touch while her mind replayed those amazing, terrifying, heady few minutes on the air mattress.

She could still feel the ghostly memory of his touch over her body, the bold way he'd taken possession, and how eagerly she'd responded to it. On shaky legs she descended back to the ground floor, and then lower into her underground study, running her hand along the wall for balance, but feeling the warm, rigid surface of Sebastian's body instead.

And every step away from him felt harder than the one before.

Muttering to herself, she lit all the candles with a wave of her hand and began pulling items off the shelves by the armful, dumping everything on the central table as echoes of sighs and moans teased her mind. Glassware clinked and clattered, books and scrolls fell off the edges, a fist-sized glass marble rolled across the floor past her toes.

Willow hardly registered any of it, her thoughts as scattered as the items she'd collected. There was some method to this madness, she was sure of it, but whenever Willow thought she knew what she was doing, her mind would flash back to her room. To Sebastian Collins.

It conjured up an intoxicating meld of memories and fantasies she couldn't block out. She saw herself entwined with him, in her bed, on the floor, in the grass beneath a bright blue, sunshiny sky. Her skin tightened at the feel of his imaginary breath, his touch, his kiss. Her hands curled around the edges of the table, aching to feel him in return, and her spine melted, needing him behind her to hold her up. To fill her up and soothe away the relentless ache of emptiness.

And none of it was real.

Willow shook herself off, looked over the heaps of stuff on her main worktable. Books and scrolls on raw magic and hexes. She arranged those to one side, shifted glassware to the center, and the herbs and tonics to the opposite end.

Order restored.

Strong hand cupping her breast, squeezing through too many maddening layers of cloth and wool. Expert lips trailing over her chin, her throat, behind her ear. Fingers clutching at her hair...

"Arrgh!" Why couldn't she stop thinking about it?

Because you lost your mind and ruined everything, possibly forever.

Willow hung her head, gazing at the scarred surface of her worktable without seeing it at all. A hard tug inside her chest made her face the door as she imagined herself reversing her trek back up to her bedroom where Sebastian was sleeping. The pull was so powerful, her feet moved in that direction, ready to obey the curse's relentless mandate as her hands reached for the laces of her gown.

She caught at their frayed ends and clutched them tightly. Gods, how could she have made such a terrible mistake? She must have miscalculated Sebastian's strength; he'd shaken off her sleep spell far too quickly. But Willow had never imagined...

Didn't matter now. What was done was done, and she couldn't undo it the same way.

Firm lips stealing her breath away, a solid weight gloriously pinning her down. The scent of him—sunshine and sex. Gods, the feel *of him. So beautifully, invitingly warm, and strong, and capable...*

Willow had taken two steps toward the door before she stopped herself. Breathing hard, she clutched the edge of her worktable to ground herself, then stubbornly turned back to the task at hand. She had to fix this before it got any worse.

If Sebastian found out, he'd hate her forever, and he'd have every right to.

Beautiful, trusting eyes turning cold…

Willow picked up the biggest tome out of the stack and opened it, tracing each line of text with her fingertips to make herself focus. It didn't help. She read the same paragraph five times, and its meaning still eluded her.

Setting the tome aside, she took up the scrolls instead, scanning through one after the other.

That tug in her chest intensified.

Willow crumpled up a delicate, ancient scroll and hurled it away. Hands speared into her hair, she tugged until the skin of her forehead was stretched taut, then she closed her eyes and took a deep breath. "You can do this. You're stronger than any curse."

It was a mistake. Without physical sights to keep her grounded, her mind once again filled with fantasies. Those sighs and moans grew louder, gained a rhythm that set the beat of her heart and made her belly quiver with need so great it made small, desperate sounds slip past her lips. It was all *just there*, just out of reach, and Willow wanted to weep with frustration.

When she opened her eyes again, she was in the hallway outside of her study, heading for the stairs. With a desperate moan, she grabbed onto the wall sconce and held on for dear life. *Gods, what am I going to do?*

Once more, she forced her feet to walk her back into her study and, this time, as soon as she crossed the threshold, she slammed the door shut, locked it, and waved a hand to magically drag a heavy bookcase across it, barricading herself inside.

She turned back to her task, shoved the spell's effects to the back of her mind as best as she could, and began assembling a series of flasks and beakers. By morning, she'd either have a cure, or one hell of a migraine.

Willow hoped with every fiber of her being that it was the former.

CHAPTER 5

Sebastian woke up cold and alone, his body stiff and sore, his head throbbing like hell. At first, he didn't remember where he was, but as he looked around, bits and pieces came back to him. He was in Willow's bedroom, on an air mattress on the floor. At his feet, the doorway barred by a massive wooden beam led to the washroom he'd used yesterday to clean himself and wash his pants—after coming in them harder than he had in memory. And just thinking about it made him half hard again.

After so many years, the feeling of physical arousal felt so foreign, he didn't know what to do with it. It gave him hope for a full recovery, but the more he thought about it, the more Sebastian realized how utterly the curse had defined him. He didn't know who he was without it; had no idea what he liked, or disliked, or what he might want to do when he didn't have to schedule his life around periodic, life-sustaining, impersonal fucks.

But last night with Willow hadn't felt impersonal. It'd felt like the fulfillment of a fervent fantasy he'd never known he had. For a few minutes, with his mind still half-mired in sleep, he'd been able to forget about everything and just *feel—everything*. Every breath and sigh. Every touch, every kiss. Even the frustration of too many clothed had invigorated him in ways he hadn't thought possible anymore. Having Willow in his arms had been a fucking revelation; a teasing hint of something beautiful, and intense, and finally within reach.

And just like that, his half-revved engine kicked into full gear, making him almost painfully hard. He wanted it all again, and more. He wanted to strip Willow of every thread and inhibition; trace every inch of her body head to toe; just…enjoy her for the sole reason that he wanted to, and it felt good. And Sebastian knew it would feel so fucking good.

The room was empty. Willow's bed looked untouched, and he didn't hear any sounds coming from the washroom. With a groan, he got up to check, just in case. He pushed open the door and ducked in under the beam. No one there.

He closed door behind him and headed for the water basin. The simple act of walking caused so much friction his legs felt weak by the time he braced himself against the wall. He stood there for a moment, watching water flow from the end of a pipe into the basin built into the wall. It had no shut-off valve and only one temperature: ice cold.

Sebastian filled his hands with it and splashed it over his face until his hands went numb and his face stung with the cold, but his relentless throbbing erection wouldn't subside. Casting a furtive glance at the closed door that had no lock, he undid his pants.

His hands were so cold, taking hold of his cock should have made it go down. Instead, it felt like a shot of aphrodisiac that somehow caused his entire body to wake up and pay attention. His weight shifted to the balls of his feet, his hips curled forward, and his cock twitched, eager for attention.

Sebastian squeezed it lightly at the base, experimenting with different pressure points as he stroked up and down. He soaped up both of his hands for lubrication, then set back in, slow, then fast, then harder, then hardly touching at all. He cupped his scrotum, played with his balls, hunched his back over the sink like a fucking pervert, jerking off in Willow's washroom where she could walk in on him at any moment.

The thought of it made his balls pull up tighter, and he pumped his fist harder, closing his eyes to imagine that. He imagined her there with him, watching him with that same all-consuming focus she'd shown his curse yesterday; imagined her catching her lower lip between her teeth and her hand slipping between her own legs—

Ah, fuck!

Sebastian shuddered through a violent wave of pleasure that wrung spurt after spurt of semen from him with such force it almost sent him to his knees. He caught himself on his elbows and thumped his forehead against the wall while he caught his breath. It put his cock so close to the water he could feel its chill against the head, making it twitch.

When he finally came back to his senses, Sebastian flushed, embarrassed and more than a little confused. That made two spine-curling orgasms in the last twenty-four hours. And both centered on Willow.

He cleaned himself up, washed away any evidence of what he'd done, half expecting to find Willow standing at the door when he turned around.

She wasn't there. And not in the bedroom, either. Now he was starting to get worried. Where the hell had she spent the night? She'd said herself the rest of this ruin wasn't habitable, and the kitchen fire wouldn't have been sufficient to keep her warm.

Newly defined dislike: Worrying about Willow's well-being.

Baffling, incomprehensible Willow, with her cool skin that somehow made him hotter than a brothel of eager women. Awkward, confusing Willow, who had no concept of proper social etiquette, which inexplicably intrigued him even more.

Willow—his host, and the only chance Sebastian would ever have of being rid of a lifelong torment, and the woman who probably wouldn't hesitate to kick him out on his ass if she knew he'd defiled her washroom. Sebastian had to get his shit together. His life was literally in Willow's hands now; he couldn't afford to fuck this up.

The screen on his phone, when he activated it, read 10:34 AM. No signal up here. Time to go find Willow. Once he'd dressed in layers and stuffed his feet into shoes, he proceeded with utmost caution out the door, conscious of the many death traps that awaited on the other side.

To his surprise, the hallway wasn't pitch black. Despite there being no windows whatsoever, holes in the walls let in enough weak sunlight to illuminate his path, and he managed to reach the stairway and make it down to the main level without breaking a leg.

"Willow?"

She wasn't in the kitchen or the entry hall. Shivering, he crossed to what had to have served as a ballroom back in the day. Now it was empty, cavernous, with nothing but torn bits of tapestries hanging on the walls, the massive fireplace spewing out a frozen mountain of ice and snow.

"Willow!" His voice bounced around, coming right back to him, but the echoes were…off somehow. Their natural rhythm was disrupted, and they kept going for much longer than he'd expect, almost like the castle itself was speaking back to him.

Thoroughly unnerved, he went back to the kitchen. There, at least, Willow had a good-sized fire burning and food of some sort cooking in the pot.

The door slammed open, startling him. Powerful winds swept through the tiny kitchen, instantly banking the fire and carrying in an inch-thick covering of snow along with a moving, creaking figure of icy fur. The figure spun around, gripping the door right back to force it closed, but its big feet slipped on the snowy floor, and the wind made the task nigh impossible.

Sebastian rushed to help, shouldering the portal closed so the figure could latch it firmly in place. Muffled sounds came out from behind the layers of fur as the figure stomped around, shaking off the snow and ice before tugging thick mittens off its hands. The impenetrable fur hood with only an inch-wide slit to see through came off next and Willow took a deep breath.

"Take *that*, you ingrates!" She shook her gloved fist, then kicked the door for good measure.

"Uh, what's going on?"

Willow blinked at him. "Oh. Hello. I didn't see you there."

Tickled by a brush of wry humor, he raised an eyebrow. "You mean through the layers of… What is that, anyway? Polar bear fur?"

She pulled her thinner gloves off. "Snow beast. Their hide is so tough it can't be cut with a knife. You need obsidian to get through it, and a magical golden needle to sew it into garments. But they last *forever.*"

Newly-defined like: women who wore snow beast fur with boundless enthusiasm.

Chuckling, Sebastian helped her undo the hooks holding the massive coat closed. He had no idea how she could even move in the thing—it was at least five inches thick and as heavy as a suit of armor. The coat hung down to her thighs, and beneath it, she wore pants made from the same material. When he set the layers on the chair, it creaked.

Sufficiently mobile now, Willow removed the slings and bags she'd strapped to her body, setting them down on the table. Each was filled with a different kind of fruit, vegetable, or herb.

Another like: women who displayed rational practicality. Even if it looked absolutely ridiculous.

"What's going on out there? Should I brace for the end of the world?"

Willow scoffed. "Hardly. It's the ice fey chieftain. He didn't like how our conversation ended yesterday, so he decided to cut me off from my summer garden." The grin she turned on him was as wicked as it was feverish. "He has no idea who he's dealing with."

It hit him like a sledgehammer to the head. One second, he was watching this odd waif of a woman push skeins of feathery gray hair out of her face, and the next he couldn't think of anything other than kissing that reckless grin from her lips. He couldn't move from the spot; couldn't tear his gaze away.

Then his hands were reaching up, adjusting her glasses farther up her nose, skimming her soft, flushed cheeks. His thumb brushed over her lower lip, and he could almost taste it already, memories of last night still so fresh in his mind his cock started to harden yet again.

Willow seemed equally entranced. Her dark brown eyes, big and round behind her glasses, stared at him without blinking, drawing him in like a vortex he couldn't escape. He reached out an inch farther to touch her hair, and his elbow popped painfully, eliciting a wince from both of them.

With the spell broken, Willow's expression became one of concern. "Are you in pain?"

"No," he lied, earning himself a scowl as he sat at the table. "Okay, maybe a little."

Newly established dislike: being denied something he craved.

That Sebastian felt well enough to have a craving at all was such a mind-bending miracle he couldn't process it.

"When did it start?" In full healer mode, Willow breezed around the kitchen, putting away the fruits of her summer garden to clear the table, relighting the fire, checking the stew pot, sweeping away the snow she'd tracked in.

Another dislike: impersonal, distracted Willow.

"Hard to tell. Woke up stiff again." *In more ways than one.* His condition had deteriorated since then, making him wonder if he was hallucinating; if his mind had finally broken so much, it had begun to translate pain into pleasure.

Or could the short respite have come because he'd made Willow orgasm last night?

Sebastian sucked in a breath, his body tightening at the memory of her writhing beneath him, eyes closed and lips parted on a plea-sured cry. Fuck, he wanted to hear it again. His hands curled into white-knuckled fists on his knees under the table where she wouldn't see, and he raised his toes off the ground so he wouldn't be tempted to stand up and push her against the wall. Or make a return trip to her washroom.

"Where do you feel it most now?"

In my balls. "Joints." It came out hoarse with his mouth dry as dust. "You never came back last night." He regretted the words before they'd even finished leaving his mouth. *Way to sound like a fucking stalker, Collins.*

"I was working on an indirect solution to your problem. In the form of a potion."

"All night?" What the fuck? That wasn't what he'd meant to say.

"Yes," she answered, then growled a little. "Where is it?"

"You stayed up all night, and you're whirring around here like a dust devil. What'd you take?"

"Wakeweed." Not even a hesitation, as if she had no verbal filters of any kind. Which was typical in people who overdosed on the herb: boundless energy, ungoverned thought processes, rapid speech, all followed by a sudden, coma-like crash.

And for all those reasons, "Wakeweed is illegal."

She scoffed. "Since when? *Aha!* Found it."

With a giddy, triumphant wiggle, she brandished the earthen bottle as high as her arm could reach. By now, the potion had had several hours to set and cool and should be ready to administer.

Facing Sebastian, she found him frowning at her. "Are you feeling all right?"

"I feel amazing!" She was winning. Not just against the ice fey, but Sebastian's curse, too. That nasty little ball of magic stood no chance against her!

"Uh-huh." He didn't sound convinced.

Oh, who cared? Willow had developed a cure for a complex structure curse overnight! She all but danced over to the cupboard across from her to retrieve an old measuring cup with the units chafed off. After a quick one-handed rinse, while her other hand still held the potion bottle, she brought both over to the table and poured Sebastian a precise measurement of thick, clear liquid.

Hmm, was it supposed to be clear, after all the ingredients she'd used? Snatching the cup back, she poured the contents into the bottle again, closed it, and shook it vigorously before pouring again. This time, the clear, thick liquid had tiny little sparks of multicolored light floating around in it. *Beauty...*

She pushed the cup in front of Sebastian. "Drink."

"What is it?"

"It's the cure," she informed him excitedly, bouncing on her feet. "Drink! You're not drinking."

"I'm having a hard time trusting your judgment right now."

Willow frowned. "Why?"

"Because you literally can't stand still. How much wakeweed did you take?"

She shrugged. "A sprig or two."

Sebastian gaped. "You're not supposed to take more than a leaf at a time."

"What's your point?"

He took a deep breath, then let it out slowly as he pushed the cup back toward her. "Okay, set the bottle down."

She did.

"Take a seat."

She sat.

"Now give me your hands."

"Why?" she asked, already placing her hands in his.

"It's an old trick my healer friend taught me. By stimulating a specific pressure point in the wrist, you reactivate your body's sleep regulation system and essentially counteract the effects of wakeweed."

"No!" She snatched her hands away again. "I can't sleep now, I have work to do! What if the potion doesn't work? And even if it does, it'll only deactivate the curse; I'll still have to pull it out manually, and then find a way to dispose of it because it won't decompose, otherwise it would have years ago, and there's the ice fey to deal with, and a harvest I haven't finished and—"

She slammed into Sebastian in front of the fire where she'd been pacing. The magical tether between them strummed hard. Willow's gaze focused on the side of his neck; she watched it move as he spoke, but none of his words registered past the ringing in her ears.

I did good, she wanted to say, but couldn't form the words. *I resisted the pull all night, and I made that potion...* She was doing good, godsdammit! Making amends; making *progress.*

So why couldn't she catch her breath? Why couldn't she think of anything other than licking that place where she could see Sebastian's heartbeat in his neck? Why was her body shivering with need for his touch?

His arm came around her waist, pulling her into his body—just as well, too, since her knees had started to buckle. She rested her chin against his shoulder, dizzy with a feverish thrill at being held this way. His lips brushed her temple, more words spoken into her hair. Willow reached up to grab hold of his shoulders for balance, but instead of holding on, her fingers pressed into his muscles in an exploring massage, and she reveled in the feel of him, so firm and steady, solid without being too hard. Just right.

Sebastian caught one of her hands, brought it to his mouth to kiss her palm as his thumb caressed her wrist, brushing back and forth lightly at first, then harder, making her lightheaded and so…so… sleepy…

Sebastian held Willow tight as she went limp in his arms, gritting his teeth against the sharp spikes of pain in his bones where they flared into joints.

Bracing against more agony, he bent to hook his arm under her knees, picking her up. She was utterly unresponsive, so deep in sleep, she wouldn't notice if all of Helegert Keep tumbled down around her ears.

One painful step at a time, Sebastian carried his lovely, *insane* burden up to her bedroom and laid her on her bed. Her hair was braided again, haphazardly at best, slipping out in a tousled halo. The attempt at restraint looked sexier than any "bedhead" hairstyle he'd ever seen before, and he still hated it. Hated that she felt she had to make the effort.

Sitting on the edge of her bed, he tugged the thong off the end of her braid and unraveled it, spreading her locks over the pillow, combing his fingers through them. The act soothed some of his irritation; her hair felt like downy feathers against his skin, a luxurious caress he shouldn't be indulging in the first place. Sebastian couldn't seem to help himself. Never would he have considered himself a hair guy.

But after a while, the strain of it started to take its toll. His already sore bones began to ache in earnest, his joints stiffening and creaking with pain. The curse was making its presence known again, reminding him he wasn't free of it yet.

Odd, though, it usually didn't come on this strong this quickly. He'd gone from almost no pain at all to barely moving in the course of a morning. At this rate, he'd be in crippling agony by tomorrow. It was time to visit Icerton's brothel. Better now than later, when he might not be able to make the trip.

Willow would sleep for a while after her wakeweed binge. He'd probably be back long before she woke up. Still, he was uneasy leaving her in this state alone for so long. Someone should be here in case she had a bad reaction or needed something.

His chest felt funny at the thought of her waking up to an empty castle again. Rubbing at it, Sebastian forced himself to his feet and away from the bed to retrieve his warm winter layers. The storm didn't sound like it'd be letting up any time soon, which meant it'd be one hell of a shitty ride to Icerton and back, but there was no help for it.

Appropriately bundled up, he headed out the door, but paused, frowning back at Willow's sleeping form. What had she meant down in the kitchen earlier, about making amends?

CHAPTER 6

The dream version of Helegert echoed with whispers that had no place in the frozen keep. Willow ran through empty, dilapidated hallways and the deeper she went, the more the keep restored itself. Walls straightened and rebuilt and the sunken roof raised up to its original position. Dust swirled outward, disappearing into the walls as colorful tapestries rolled down from their moorings. Bright crystal chandeliers grew like roots down from the ceiling, sconces sprouted from the walls.

"Willow..."

Strong arms came around her, whirling her into the ballroom and a smooth, twirling waltz. Willow looked up into her partners face. "Sebastian?"

He smiled, then twirled her away before pulling her back into his arms. They danced a circuit around the ballroom, staring into each other's eyes, and the butterflies in Willow's belly scattered into every inch of her body.

She leaned closer into Sebastian's embrace, clutching his shoulders. The fabric of his formal coat gave way as the sleeves separated from the shoulders, sliding down his arms, and he released her one arm at a time just long enough to get rid of them. When he clutched her hip once more, the same happened with her skirts—they melted from her so easily...

The floor bloomed into a plush carpet beneath her feet. Heat from a good-sized fire warmed her bare back. She heard water trickling down one wall, steaming up the room until a soft haze enveloped her.

She pressed against Sebastian, wanting to melt into him forever. This was what she'd been missing. "I never knew... Oh!" Sebastian lifted her up, guided her legs around his hips, his hard member sliding naturally between the lips of her sex. The friction was beyond anything she'd ever felt before. Sharp, intense, yet soothing, almost loving at the same time.

She blinked and found herself sinking deep into a mattress made of clouds, arching up to Sebastian, desperately needing him inside her; she felt incomplete when he wasn't touching her, and terrified that if he stopped, he'd disappear, and she'd never be whole again.

"Please," she breathed, her body poised on the very edge of some cataclysmic event she wanted to dive into headlong. "Please..."

Sebastian stroked her breasts, her belly, her hips, worshipping her with every kiss and caress, driving her out of her mind with over-whelming sensation, and all the while the length of him slid up and down across her sex. So close... So...

A sharp stab of pain in her chest made her cry out. Sebastian reared away, searching her gaze with a worried frown. A silent question passed his lips, and Willow couldn't answer. She couldn't even take a breath when her ribs felt as if they'd just shattered all at once. The pain radiated down her spine, out into her limbs, and in her mind, she screamed and screamed, but no sound would come out.

Sebastian cupped her face, made her look at him, appearing pained for her sake. He kissed the top of her head, then melted away, and with him, all of Helegert disappeared, too.

Now she was standing in the corner of a dank, cold room, the floor-boards and walls creaking with the force of a wind that rocked the little building at its very foundation. The hearth fire was almost out; there was no more wood to put on it. And in the bed, a pale woman with garish lipstick smeared across her mouth lay back and spread her legs, her empty eyes staring straight through the lover coming to her.

Willow wailed as the pain brought her to her knees, just as the man appeared to fall to his own on the edge of the bed. He shuddered, his head hung as he breathed it down, then advanced on his lover.

"Sebastian...no..."

He couldn't hear her. His hands touched the empty woman almost desperately, fingers curled as if he couldn't straighten them—neither could Willow. Somehow, his torment was hers, and she felt it all. The disgust, the helplessness, the cold detachment with which he touched the woman, needing to please her to save himself.

It didn't work. Took too much time, too much effort. He could hardly move, and the woman knew it. She didn't respond the way he needed her to.

With a pained roar, Sebastian rolled sideways, shivering on the edge of the bed as the woman stared at him in petrified silence. She touched him, and he flinched away, and so did Willow, screaming his agony for him. It was killing him—and her right along with him...

Strong hands shook her. "Willow, wake up."

She groaned, frowning in sleep. Her body felt so heavy it seemed impossible that she could ever move it again, but the voice was harsh, insistent, and filled with pain. Willow forced her eyes open, squinting at the blur above her. "Wha?"

Sebastian sat her up, slid her glasses onto her nose, and the world sprang into focus. "Are you up?" he asked, his face pinched with pain.

Still fuzzy and tired, Willow nodded.

"Good. I need you to do whatever you did my first night here." He broke off to take a sharp breath. "Please."

Roused into action, Willow threw back the covers and lurched to her feet. "Lie down." Her body was slow to move, her mind slow to engage, but necessity kept her moving; guilt adding a feeble spring in her step. "What happened?" she asked as Sebastian lowered himself to the mattress, his movements slow, his breathing reduced to quick, shallow pants, and his teeth gritted against the pain. Adjusting her sight, she looked for the yarn ball of his curse and instead found a blinding starburst spinning madly inside him, the sharp points cutting across bones, muscles, and organs.

"Pain started up again," he said haltingly. "Rode to Icerton. Tried. Usual remedy. Didn't help." He groaned, his breath turning choppy. "Please... If you. Can't help... Kill me."

"Oh gods…" *Don't panic. Don't panic! DON'T PANIC!*

"Please…" He could barely speak, as if his jaw was wired shut, and he hadn't twitched since lying down.

Willow's hands shook as she unbuttoned his shirt and pulled the sides apart. Digging her nails into the fabric of his pullover under-shirt, she ripped it down the middle, then laid her palms flat against his chest. His skin was cold, but underneath it, his flesh burned with the curse's effects, and she perceived something else that chilled her to her very soul.

If she couldn't break the curse, here and now, Sebastian Collins would die by sunset.

I'm panicking!

With a groan, Sebastian caught hold of her hand and squeezed. "Please."

"I'm sorry," she whispered. "Yes, of course, I'll help."

Drawing on every ounce of her strength, she plunged her con-sciousness straight into the deadly vortex to its very heart. Applying lash after lash of magical binding, she tied it up in clumsy knots until its spin began to slow. Nowhere near defeated, the sharp spikes shot out longer, stabbing farther, and somewhere in the distance, she thought she heard Sebastian scream. It lashed at her, too. Willow took the pain; let it pass through her because she knew if she tried to resist or evade, it would stick to her like glue.

With the core sealed, only the aggressive spikes poked out of the bundle she'd created. Willow had hold of the curse now; she could pull it out. But with those spikes embedded so deep, the process might well kill him. An impossible choice.

Sebastian's nails dug into her wrist, reminding her he was still there, still suffering unimaginable agonies.

Willow gritted her teeth, bore down, and yanked as hard as she could.

The curse squealed as it tore free of Sebastian's body. Like a mad, living thing, its sharp points turned into lash-like tentacles, snapping and flailing as it searched for a new place to anchor itself.

Willow spun it, winding the tentacles back onto itself, adding more binds among them and over them, until the entire thing was coated in a thick layer of her will. But raw magic wasn't that easy to defeat. Like any other energy, it could be neither created, nor destroyed, only reshaped and repurposed. After so many years of its only purpose being to cause as much pain as possible, it'd take years more to reshape it—a much larger task than she could undertake at present.

For the moment, she conjured a blob of molten glass to encase it, then sent it deep into the ground beneath Helegert to keep it contained. There it settled, squealing furiously as if it were a sentient thing. Its voice was loud enough that Willow still heard it after she broke off from it, like an endless subliminal echo that wouldn't stop.

That couldn't be good.

On the bed, Sebastian's body had gone lax. His eyes were closed, and he looked to be sleeping but, still connected to him, Willow knew he was very much awake, waiting for the other shoe to drop. She took quick inventory of his anatomy and found no lasting damage. Physically, at least, he was back to full strength.

"Sebastian?"

He groaned.

"H-how do you feel?"

He opened his jaw wide, then closed it. "Better."

"Can you move?"

He shifted his shoulders up and down, rolled his wrists, then his elbows, then pulled his knees in and pushed himself up to sit. Rolling his head on his shoulders, he finally faced her, breathing out a harsh sigh. "Still sore, but I can move." Despite his obvious relief, his eyes were still wary. "What's the prognosis?"

Willow sat back on her heels, focused her sight to see magic and scanned Sebastian from head to toe. His entire being sparkled with the remnants of her power, but not a single particle of the curse remained. There was only a dark hollow, a vacuum left behind by the curse's magical presence, but it was already filling in with—

She gasped, broke away, and barely prevented herself from jumping off the bed.

"Willow? What is it?"

Within moments, the hollow was filled, and his aura reformed into its natural state.

Except…

Sebastian sat up, caught her hands in his to break her stare. "Willow, talk to me."

She blinked up at him. "All good," she said, forcing a smile, even as her eyes refused to blink. "Turns out, the curse was most vulnerable when it was most active. It's gone now."

He frowned. "Then why am I still sore?"

"Echoes," she replied. Not exactly a lie. "You'll probably feel the after effects for some time, but they should fade eventually." Unlike that other thing…

Sebastian's frown cleared. He grinned at her, looking so gods-damned beautiful Willow hated herself for lying to him. "You really did it. I can't believe it." He squeezed her hands, brought them up to his mouth, and kissed each one. "Words will never be enough, but thank you, Willow."

"You're welcome." *I'm so sorry,* she added in her thoughts, staring at the new quaff of magic now nestled in the center of his chest, and the tether that bound it to her own, now ten times thicker and much, much more powerful.

CHAPTER 7

With echoes of the pain still humming in his bones, Sebastian went through the motions of washing all traces of a cheap brothel off his body, his head still spinning from the sudden change in his fortunes.

He'd been so sure he'd reached the end of the line, riding hell for leather through a snowstorm in the worst throes of the curse.

Gods, he hadn't felt so close to death in years. The last time…

Sebastian shuddered at the memory.

The last time, he'd almost gotten Snow White killed. Because he'd been a careless fool, the war had almost ended before Snow had even had a chance to turn the tide. She should have cut off his head for it—she'd had the right, and the opportunity. Instead, the young, virginal queen-to-be had somehow saved his life. "We need never speak of this, if you wish it," she'd said the next day. "But know that I regret nothing. And you are still not free of your duty to me."

Humbled, and overcome with gratitude, he'd eagerly knelt before his queen and renewed his oath of fealty then and there, adding another to himself that he would never again do anything to jeopardize her life.

And he never had.

As much as it shamed him that she'd been forced into that situation, the fact that he'd been able to serve her faithfully and effectively all the years since brought Sebastian at least a small sense of pride. But that he'd somehow managed to cultivate and retain a friendship with Valefort's true queen on top of that still boggled his mind.

To this day, Snow had never spoken of that night or hinted at what she'd done.

To this day, Sebastian had never asked.

All he knew was that she'd somehow managed to stave off his death then, and, by sending him here to Helegert, she'd saved his life for good. Which meant it now belonged to her. And that meant he had a task to complete.

"Willow?"

She jumped, squinted at the blur that was Sebastian. "Huh?"

"Are you all right?"

Willow adjusted her spectacles and looked around. She was sitting at the kitchen table, her face burning from where she'd rested it in her hands. *Did I fall asleep?* She must have. Exhaustion still weighed on her like a ton of dirt from her wakeweed crash. If Sebastian hadn't woken her, she probably would have slept the day away. "Yes, 'm fine. Just a little tired. How are you?"

He rolled his shoulder and winced. "Still sore. But I'll live." Another one of those brilliant smiles lit up his face. "Thanks to you."

She vacated the seat so he wouldn't see the pathetic grimace of a smile she attempted in return. "Sit, please."

Gingerly, he did, but it seemed to be more out of habit than actual pain. When he was settled, Sebastian sighed with a mixture of relief and pleasure, and the small sound twanged the tether between them, yanking her closer to him. The urge to sit on his lap was so powerful, Willow found herself shuffling closer, staring hard at his crotch.

Even as tired as she was, the temptation to strip off her clothes and launch herself at him was so powerful her hands clutched at her dress. She felt overheated, light-headed, and quivery all over, aching deep between her legs where she could almost feel Sebastian already. Her body responded to the merest thought of him sliding in and out of her, hard and thick, rocking her back and forth with the power of his thrusts—

When he looked over at her, she quickly tore her gaze away and forced her body back under control. "I have something that might help the soreness." She rooted through the cupboards. "It should go away on its own eventually, but why endure more pain when you don't have to, yes?" Where had she put that potion yesterday? It had to be here somewhere… "After all, you've already had more than enough for a lifetime. I'm surprised your hair hasn't gone as gray as mine…" *Awkward subject. Avoid.*

"Are you sure you're all right?"

Her sex clenched at the sound of his voice and Willow had to bite back a moan. "Perfectly fine. Ah! Here it is."

"Very well, then there's something I'd like to talk to you about."

Willow shook the potion bottle before pouring another dose. "Oh?"

"Queen Snow… That is—*ahem*—what I mean is—"

"Here we go." She offered the cup in both hands, staring hard at its contents so she wouldn't have to look at him. Her body all but screamed at her to straddle his lap, help him drink. Her legs half buckled with the need to obey, but she resisted, her face heating with the effort. Sebastian was a good man; he didn't deserve this kind of manipulation.

"Is this the same stuff you tried to make me drink yesterday?"

"Yes," she breathed, holding it out closer to his face as she silently willed her body not to follow.

"The 'potion' you made while under the influence of massive amounts of wakeweed?"

She frowned into his skeptical eyes. "Why do you say it like that?" Talking about magic helped her focus on something other than the throbbing ache at her core that made her desperate for contact of any kind, even if it was her own hand. "Wakeweed doesn't alter the way one thinks, only allows them more continuous time to do it."

"So you can tell me every ingredient that went into this, its inherent properties, and how it interacts with the others?"

"Absolutely." More or less. "The majority of them are healing herbs enhanced with raw magic, and there's another component of…of… Well, I can't think of the name right now, but I know what it does."

"Which is what?"

Makes me want to lick all over your body, taste the salt of your skin, make you come on my tongue… She shook her head. "Humor me, will you? Please?"

He made a face at her.

"I did save your life, remember? You trusted me that much an hour ago, but you won't trust me now?"

Sebastian stared a moment longer, then put his hands over hers on the cup and brought it to his lips. Holding her gaze the entire time, he tipped the cup up and took a drink.

Willow forgot to breathe. She swayed on her feet, watching his throat work on a swallow. He hadn't shaved. How would the dark bristle shadowing his jaw feel against her cheek? Her thighs? She pressed her knees together as the cup slipped free of his lips. "There. Are you happy now?"

"Yes," she managed to reply. "Thank you." But when she would have pulled away, his hold on her hands—and the cup—tightened, keeping her in place. He brought it to his lips for one more drink, and this time, the way he looked at her made Willow so weak in the knees she leaned deeper forward than was necessary. She couldn't look away as he drank down the cup's contents.

The tether between them hummed with an almost physical sound that compelled Willow to do its bidding. Already, she stood so close one of his legs was completely hidden in her skirts. A step closer and she'd be standing between his legs, and she wanted to be there; needed to feel his body against hers the way she had in her dream.

Sebastian, too, had to feel its effects. The cup was empty now, but he retained his hold on it—and her—keeping her close, his thumbs brushing back and forth across her knuckles as her shoulders hunched, bringing her face lower over his. The will of the magic she'd inevitably wrought was not to be denied.

And it wasn't fair.

It wasn't real.

Somehow, Willow forced herself away from him; put the width of half the kitchen between them as she rinsed the cup in cold water and put it back in its place. "Would you like a tour of Helegert Keep today?" She almost dropped the cup inches from the cupboard. Where in the world had that come from?

"Yes, I'd like that," he replied, sounding dazed.

"Good." That ought to keep them busy for a while. The keep was immense and, although much of it was in ruin, its history was fascinating, to say the least.

And as long as Willow kept her mind on that, perhaps she could even stop herself doing something else she'd never be able to take back.

CHAPTER 8

Sebastian followed Willow out of the kitchen, in a daze. He'd been skeptical about that "potion" of hers, but for a moment after he'd taken his first sip, his aches had actually lessened, just as she'd promised they would.

But then he'd felt this powerful…*something* take root inside of him, like an irresistible force that pulled him toward Willow. Sebastian hadn't been able to tear his gaze away, noticing things he hadn't before. Like the way her brown eyes sparkled with an amber sort of underglow, or the way her hair, in different lighting, seemed almost white. Or the delicate softness of her skin.

He'd gone instantly, inexplicably hard, and all he'd been able to think about had been pulling Willow between his knees, threading his fingers into her hair, and kissing those soft lips again. He'd still had the taste of her on his tongue, even as he'd drunk the witch's brew she'd served him. She'd been so close, so hauntingly focused on him, he could have pulled her onto his lap and basked in her forever.

And then, in an instant, she'd turned away, that feeling had disappeared, and his aches had come right back again. He'd felt as if he'd somehow…displeased her. But that couldn't be right.

"This used to be called the Hall of Echoes," Willow was saying.

They were in the great chamber he'd gone through yesterday, looking for her. "In Helegert's glory days, this was where they would hold grand balls. The musicians had to be specially trained to play *with* the acoustics, and if they did it right, the melody they played built on itself and seemed endless. Have you ever stood between two mirrors slightly askew?"

"Where you see an endless corridor of your own reflections? Yes." And he'd always found it profoundly unnerving.

"Exactly," she told him with a bright smile that shot right to his cock. "It was like that, only with music."

"Then I'm glad I wasn't here to see it," he retorted.

Willow laughed, the echoes returning her exuberance tenfold and, somehow, his step lightened, some of the strain easing from his joints. Maybe that potion had worked, after all.

They walked through chambers completely destroyed by war and neglect, passed by some that could no longer even be opened, and some that hadn't been damaged at all, except by the passage of time. At each stop, Willow's lilting voice painted pictures in Sebastian's mind, of what the keep must have looked like back when it'd been the crown jewel of White Plains.

He listened with drowsy enjoyment, smiling at Willow's obvious joy at having someone to share all this history with. Her love of this place bled into the passionate words she spoke, and the dreamy looks she cast around her. Once in a while, she'd point out a detail or feature, reaching up to his arm to get his attention, but she never quite… connected. Her hand always hovered a fraction of an inch over the surface of his shirt in a ghost of a caress that always felt like static electricity against his skin.

If he'd suspected she was trying to use her wiles on him, he'd call her out for the deliberate tease, but that didn't seem to be the case. It felt more like Willow didn't know *how* to physically interact with another person. In many ways, she was like a wildling child who'd been taught the theory of proper social etiquette, but not its practical application.

But she was trying, and that spirit, coupled with her mind-boggling intellect, had Sebastian entranced for hours, long after he should have been bored out of his mind. And long after his body should have given out, forcing him to rest, he was still chasing at her heels, feeling better than he ever had in memory. Sebastian hung on every word she spoke, feeling *happy*.

"And this was the master wing," Willow said, stopping in an arch-way made narrow by fallen boulders and debris, several feet away from the crumbling stairs that led up to her bedroom. Voice hushed, as if imparting a secret, she confided, "No visitors were ever allowed up there, unless expressly invited by the lady of the keep." Crooking a finger, she beckoned him closer and, charmed down to the marrow of his bones, Sebastian leaned in to put his ear at her mouth. "Rumor has it," she whispered, "that the keep's original mistress had many lovers, sometimes enjoying several in one evening, but they never knew about each other."

"How?" he whispered back, his mouth skimming the outer rim of her ear.

Willow shivered, her voice turning breathy. "It was said that the keep had hidden doorways and secret passages, and when the mis-tress was finished with one lover, she'd send him off through one passage, and admit the next through another."

Her back was to the wall and, standing this close to her, Sebastian could put his hands on it on either side of her and have her neatly trapped. He could keep her there for hours, with his head buried between her legs, feasting on her until she begged him to stop. Then he'd take her against that wall until they were both too tired to move. Sebastian became so wrapped up in that fantasy, imagining Willow's cool hands clutching at him, her long, lithe limbs going boneless with pleasure, he forgot why it would all be a very bad idea.

He pulled back enough to see her blush, her red lips parted in invitation.

Sebastian did put his hands on that wall, for balance more than anything else, but even as he leaned his weight on them to stay up-right, his elbows bent to bring him closer, and his lips brushed hers just barely. Just a whisper of a touch, like all of hers were.

Even that brief contact sent a jolt through his body, started his heart pumping hard and fast. His fingers curled against the wall, the tips digging into a crease between two stones, anchoring him to rock so he wouldn't be tempted to touch her, because if he started, Sebastian didn't think he'd have the strength of will to stop. He wanted to touch her so much his entire being rebelled at the careful distance he managed to maintain.

He imagined kissing her so hard he forgot to breathe, devouring bit by bit. Sebastian knew she'd match him—for all her quirks, Willow wasn't shy. She'd tear at his clothes and clutch her legs around him, and she'd be so wet for him, begging him to take her—

"I thought you said you weren't interested in sex," she whispered in a lover's croon.

It took Sebastian a moment to register the words. He tensed, pulling back, but couldn't seem to make himself step away altogether. Some invisible force had him in a tangle, thoroughly lashed to Willow and fighting it felt like a battle against himself. One he didn't even want to win. "I wasn't," he replied softly, then shook himself and added with more conviction, "I'm not. I mean… I'm not sure…"

The idea of it had never appealed to him before. For most of his life, sex had been nothing but an abhorrent act of self-preservation. But everything was different now. In the span of a day, he'd gone from being resigned to his fate to having his entire life ahead of him, and it was a heady, exuberant feeling that didn't exactly lend itself to rational thought.

Was he interested in sex? In the desperate way a teenager hungered for any physical experience he could possibly get. He wanted days, weeks of the same all-consuming passion he'd felt his first night here. No rules, no restrictions, just sex. Slow, fast, hard gentle, straightforward, or crazy kinked—Sebastian didn't care. He wanted it all.

What unsettled him was how quickly he'd managed to set aside the last fourteen years of disgust at the mere thought of sex. And how thoroughly he seemed to have fixated on Willow as the subject of his newfound lust.

Even while his rational mind told him this sudden attraction made no sense, his hands itched to bury in Willow's hair and all his muscles clenched with the instinct to pick her up and get as close as physically possible, so he could feel her heartbeat against him.

And a part of him he'd thought had died long ago whispered that even that wasn't close enough.

Willow's flush deepened, and her gaze skittered sideways away from him. She didn't say another word, and he somehow sensed she didn't know *what* to say, as if she'd never been in a situation like this before, and didn't want to make everything worse.

A decidedly uncomfortable thought occurred to him. "Willow, are you a virgin?"

She shook her head.

Thank the gods. "Do I make you nervous?"

Again, she shook her head, her gaze finding his for a second, but in that second, he saw so much longing in her eyes it almost dropped him to his knees. Yet somehow she still managed to resist it. Nodding at something behind him, she said, "T-there's a secret passage over here. If you twist the sconce…"

It was the last thing Sebastian wanted to do, but he'd never taken an unwilling woman, and he wasn't about to start now. Willow wasn't ready for what he wanted from her—hell, Sebastian wasn't sure *he* was ready for it.

With the last ounce of his will, Sebastian pushed away from the wall and stepped back until his shoulder blade hit the other side of the archway. It was barely a step and a half, but even that small retreat exacted a massive cost. His legs quivered with strain, and his hand felt clumsy as he reached out sideways to twist the sconce, but he did it for the promise of a distraction, because the longer he kept looking at Willow, the more difficult it became to think of anything other than burying his cock inside her as deep as he could go.

And that same forgotten part of him whispered that even that wouldn't be deep enough.

The hallway shuddered, rocking him off balance as the hidden mechanism yanked a part of the wall inward. Dust exploded around him, obscuring his vision, but he heard the wall retract sideways and, when the dust cleared, the dark tunnel stood open.

"I haven't used this one since before my grandmother died," Willow said, joining him at the entrance. "She found me playing in the tunnel once and became so upset… I've never seen her in such a state before. For days and days, Rowena wouldn't even look at me, and her hands started shaking whenever I tried to apologize. I couldn't stand seeing her like that, so told her I would never do it again, that I didn't want to anymore—and it was the truth."

"Should we be here now?"

"What's left to be scared of?" Willow replied with an easy shrug, but she looked nervous as she weaved her hands before her, conjuring a swarm of faery lights, then, with a flick of her fingers, she sent them flying into the passage. "Only ghosts and memories down here." The lights spread out along the walls, illuminating a long, narrow hallway littered with rubble and curtained with spider webs. Taking a deep breath, Willow blew at them, and the curtains parted, flattening against the walls. "Shall we?"

"Where does it lead?"

She smiled, half mysterious, half teasing. "Let's find out."

Still far too tempted to crowd her against the wall and lift her legs around his waist, Sebastian wasn't sure of the wisdom of traipsing through a dark, narrow passageway with her, yet still heard himself ask, "Will you at least hold my hand?"

Willow hesitated, raised her hand, and then pulled it behind her back. Her lips moved soundlessly in some silent internal dialogue for a moment, and then she appeared to make a decision and took his hand, spinning away immediately to take the lead at a brisk pace.

Sebastian didn't mind. The fact that he got her to touch him of her own volition was a major win in and of itself.

Willow's ears popped as the downward sloping path dipped underground. Here, out of the wind's reach, the temperature was always stable at a comfortable level. The stone was cool to the touch, the floor gradually transitioning from smoothed rock to stomped dirt which softened any noise she and Sebastian made.

"How far are we going?" Sebastian asked, lightly squeezing her hand.

Unnervingly aware of his presence so close to her, she kept quickening her pace, somehow trying to outrun him despite his hold on her, but he hadn't complained a single time. Now, just short of jogging, Willow made a conscious effort to slow. "We're almost there."

Up ahead, a closed cage door barred any entry. She unlocked it from a few steps away with a simple bend of her will, and the door swung open on creaky hinges.

The lights she'd summoned swarmed inside, grouping together at the center of the domed ceiling. A series of mirrors mounted along the edges reflected them, bathing the chamber in warm, yellow light.

"This place is like a treasure cave," Sebastian said, releasing his hold on her as he looked around in awe.

Willow wrinkled her nose. "More like a repository of old junk."

Massive wooden chests and traveling trunks piled up along the edges of the room. Haphazard tables here and there were piled with bolts of fabric, books, old toys, and jeweled keepsake boxes. Three seamstress stands held beautiful gowns damaged by long years of neglect, their trimmings hanging loose, pearls and precious stones littering the ground beneath them.

Sebastian carefully picked his steps over to a pile of folded tapestries. He caught the edges of the topmost one and, raising it up over his head, let the fabric unfurl until its tassels swept the ground. "The royal banner of Sturmgard."

"Yes," Willow confirmed. "Probably abandoned during the war. And now I understand why Rowena didn't want me playing down here."

Sebastian's gaze finding hers and held with an unblinking intensity, as if the reason was of utmost importance to him.

Willow gave him a lopsided smile. "As a little girl, I used to pretend I was secretly a cursed princess. If I'd known all these things were here, I don't think they would have survived my rambunctious games." Her smile turned wistful. "I suppose every little girl who lives in a broken, abandoned castle dreams of being a princess."

"What if it was true?"

Chuckling, she shook her head, then looked around at all the treasures so carelessly abandoned here. "I'd be a princess of nowhere, my royal blood forgotten by time itself." Giving in to the fanciful thought, she strolled around the chamber, picking up knickknacks here and there. "My heritage would be noble and proud, but I'd be the last of my family."

"Why the last?"

She raised an eyebrow at him, gesturing around herself. "Because if I still had family, they would never have let me live here like this." *Alone.*

How many nights had she lain in bed, imagining a long lost ancestor riding in to claim her? How many times had she wished someone would come rescue Helegert from this ruin, rebuild it to its former glory, and fill it with elegant people dressed in butterfly gowns and finery? She longed so badly to hear these echoing halls filled with laughter and conversation.

When the silence stretched long, she looked back at Sebastian to find him watching her with something like pity, or regret, but not quite. He crossed the distance between them until he stood so close she had to crane her head back to hold his gaze.

That easily, her heart was set aflutter, and her mouth went dry, yearning for his kiss to give her breath. His nearness alone made her dress feel too heavy and warm. She rocked back on her heels, then up onto her toes, drawn like a magnet to his lips. Willow silently willed his hands to touch her, to relieve the aching tightness of her skin. In that moment, she needed him more than her next heartbeat.

Leaning in, Sebastian whispered, "If I asked you to come to Kesteran with me when I leave, would you?"

Leave Helegert? Never!

Yet even as she thought it, she remembered last night's wake-weed-tainted dream of Helegert crumbling behind her. Willow wasn't a superstitious sort, but that dream had unnerved her far more than she cared to admit.

Grandmother Rowena had loved to tell her faery stories about how Helegert was alive, and each Faithblade woman to be born in it became a part of it, as it became a part of her. She would tell tales of impossible feats and magical happenings that had kept their family safe and cared for within its walls for generation after generation, and each story ended with the same lesson: Take care of Helegert, and it will take care of you.

Whether she wanted it or not, Willow was part of that tradition. Helegert was part of her, as she was part of it, just as her foremothers had been, to the point where she feared her presence here was the only thing keeping the walls upright. If she left… What if Helegert really did fall? It would be her fault.

"No," she said, the simple word causing her chest to constrict in a painful spasm. "I'm afraid the good people of Icerton had it right when they dubbed me the ghoul of Helegert Keep. I'll haunt this place until I die, and forever after."

It was her duty.

CHAPTER 9

Sebastian had never seen anything as beautiful as the scene before him. Helegert's grand ballroom, with its patterned parquet floors, gold-and-mirror walls, and rich, blood red curtains framing each window and nook—all encased in a thick, glossy layer of ice. Everything glittered with magic like the inside of a jewelry box, and at its center, a raised dais sat like a massive pillow draped in pure white.

Sebastian floated toward it, and the closer he got, the more ethereal the scene became. The pillow dipped in the middle, as a form took shape upon it: long, sleek limbs, a lithe, slender body, so pale she almost blended into the white sheets, but not completely.

Willow opened her eyes, her red lips parting on a sigh. Her gray mane was paler, almost white, and each of her breaths was a puff of mist. Her hand skimmed down her body, unabashedly dipping between her legs as she stroked herself, her back arching to the sensation, her nipples beading.

Sebastian lost his breath. His body trembled at the sight of her, with anger as much as desire. How dare she take this away from him! That pleasure was his to give. Surging forward, he caught the naughty hand and stopped her ministrations.

Willow blinked as if she hadn't realized he was even in the room.

But then those red lips of hers curled wickedly, and with her free hand, she grasped his hard cock. Her touch was cold on his overheated flesh. Instead of a rub, she gave a decisive tug, pulling him onto the bed with her. Sebastian eagerly settled between her legs, groaned when she wrapped them around his hips, wrapped him in her winter's chill.

She was the sweetest kind of ice, a teasing hint of magic that could kill as easily as give life. "I want you," she whispered, her misty breath puffing against his cheeks. Her fingers, still wet with her juices, traced his lips. Sebastian opened his mouth, drew the taste of her onto his tongue, sucked it clean from her fingertips.

He bucked against her, sliding his cock between the soft lips of her sex, blindly seeking entry. He was denied. Willow shook her head, a temptress smile curving her lips. Her pale hands lit like snowflakes onto his shoulders, frost sprouting in intricate patterns around her touch, and then she pushed, guiding him down the length of her body.

"Yes!" Sebastian hissed. He traced kisses across the blue patterns blooming and fading over her torso, dipped his tongue into her navel, then pressed his mouth to the center of her abdomen as his thumbs caressed the creases of her loins.

Her legs fell open for him, her hands tunneling into his hair. She was aching for release and wasn't shy about letting him know. Sebastian smiled against her. He liked that she knew what she wanted.

But her grievous slight needed to be punished. Taking hold of her hands, he pressed them to the bed. He didn't have her kind of magic, but in this world, Helegert was as much his to command as hers. Their joined hands sank into the bed up to their wrists, and when Sebastian pulled back, Willow remained stuck.

Already half-crazed with desire, she bucked and rocked beneath him, fighting her bonds. They held her fast. She hooked her knee over his shoulder, to urge him on that way. Instead, Sebastian pressed his mouth to the inside of her knee before pushing it away, then kissed a leisurely path back up to her petite breasts, his mouth watering for the feast he was about to make of them.

He teased and tormented her until her cries echoed all around him, multiplying onto themselves like music, and the more she responded to him, the more he wanted to play. Frozen crystal chandeliers chimed, ice cracked to the rhythm as Willow writhed to his touch, dancing for him—with him. Sebastian couldn't get enough, the drive to amp up her pleasure overriding the need to achieve his own.

In that moment, Sebastian was a slave to Willow's desire.

And for one brief, delicate moment, that scared the ever living shit out of him.

"Please!" she finally shouted, her entire body taut with the tension of denied pleasure, and Sebastian relented. He slid down her body once more, delving straight for the core of her, kissing her body the same way he longed to kiss her mouth: deeply, ravenously.

Her scream of pleasure was almost soundless. Her body arched, shuddering as her juices bathed his tongue.

But she wasn't mindless. Using his own trick against him, she warped the bed, made him sink into it, the soft mattress swallowing his cock and balls, squeezing and pulling, mirroring her own orgasm. Sebastian almost came then and there.

Oh, but he wasn't anywhere near finished with her...

With her body still quivering through aftershocks, Willow slowly came back to her senses, her gaze snaring on a crystal chandelier right above her. A drop fell from the centermost crystal, splashing down onto her cheek. The sensation raised goose bumps over every inch of her skin, made her shiver as Sebastian moved up her body, hooking his elbows around the backs of her knees to tilt her hips up.

In this land of frozen beauty, his raw, hot vitality took her breath away. He was fire to her ice; melting not just her, but the world around her. Steam hissed wherever they touched, hazing the dream in sensual mist, but Willow sensed it all changing around her.

As the ice receded from the ceiling, brilliant paintings almost distracted her from Sebastian's intense gaze. She perceived that comforting layer of cold shrinking down along the walls, and from somewhere in the distance, faint strains of music whispered on the warm, summer breeze.

Too much heat—it was scorching her!

Sebastian's lips grazed her collarbone, and she cried out with equal amounts of pain and pleasure. He left her branded, and still aching for more. His hands roamed across her skin like molten iron, painting her flesh red, but the more he touched, the less she hurt, and soon, pain became pleasure, and Willow once again fought her binds, eager to touch him in return.

"For you," Sebastian whispered at her ear. "Everything for you…" He shifted above her, his eyes bright with a hunger so deep, she feared it would devour her whole, but there was something else, too…a shard of cool ice beneath the surface, like a small, bright star glittering within him, offering succor from the unbearable heat.

It was a part of her, a chip off her soul lodged inside of his, binding them together, pulling them ever toward each other.

He doesn't know.

That guilt again grew, snaking tentacles around her heart.

Sebastian's lips hovered a hair's breadth above her own, taunting with the promise of something beautifully, magically grand. "You own me, Willow…"

The head of his cock touched the core of her, pressed forward. Willow's lips parted, her breath frozen inside her as she teetered on a dangerous edge. She wanted to give in, to dive headlong toward the unknown, but fear kept her rooted in place.

"You own me," he said again, and all she could think was, No more than you me.

He sank deeper into her, then deeper still, and a little more, and all the while, he never blinked, as if this moment, this connection, was of utmost importance. As slowly as he'd advanced, Sebastian pulled back, then rocked forward again. The rhythm was like a languorous dance that soothed away everything but him.

"Kiss me," she pleaded. Feeling pleasure build inside her once more. "Please…"

He didn't.

Instead, as if roused by her wish, he picked up speed, thrusting harder and faster as the chamber heated even more. Ghosts of elegantly clad figures whirled around them in a mad waltz, spinning closer, filling the room until a wall of ever-moving bodies enclosed the bed.

With the music blaring so loud she couldn't hear her own screams, Willow fought her binds harder, a sliver of fear worming its way into her heart even as her body rocked toward Sebastian, meeting each of his thrusts, urging him on.

Sebastian never faltered, his focus absolute, and absolutely trained on her. His body responded to every twitch of hers, meeting her needs before she could voice them, but he denied her the one thing she needed more than air and ice.

"Sebastian!" Her hands broke free of the bed, and she clutched at his shoulders, his neck, grasping his hair to bring him closer, to taste his lips. She could feel it like the forgotten answer to a riddle hovering just out of reach; everything would work out if only he'd kiss her...

Sebastian buried his face in her neck, his arms snaking around her to clutch her close as he pistoned inside her so hard the entire bed jarred beneath them.

And Willow loved it.

"More!" she cried, made dizzy by the dervish of flailing skirts pressing in on her from all sides—yellow, orange, and red. Like fire...

Sebastian crossed his arms behind her back, grabbed hold of her rear, and gave her what she asked for, grinding against her until the most exquisite build-up of pleasure burst like magic inside her as the dancers around them burst into flames.

She woke with a cry on her lips, bolting upright in bed as her body shuddered through waves of pleasure, and in the darkness at the foot of her bed, Sebastian jolted awake along with her with a shout of, "What!"

"W-what?" she repeated, trying and failing to hide how out of breath she was; trying and failing to stay composed as more pleasure rocked her.

"You screamed," Sebastian said, sounding equally out of breath. "You woke me."

"No, I didn't," she lied. "You woke me."

Silence.

Groan.

"Are you in pain again?" Willow asked.

After a tense pause, Sebastian answered, "I'll live. Go back to sleep."

Could it be…?

Was it possible that Sebastian might have…?

No. Shared dreams were a myth.

But the tether between them wasn't. And even as she told herself to close her eyes and pretend nothing had happened, that it had all been a dream both of them would have forgotten long before sunrise, Willow yearned to slip out of her bed and slide into his.

You own me, Willow, his dream self had told her.

Her waking self still responded the same: *No more than you me.*

CHAPTER 10

Another bitter storm blew in the next day, stranding them in Helegert. They couldn't even reach the summer garden to collect produce. Sebastian's bones still buzzed from last night's dream. Never mind that his entire body felt like his marrow had been replaced by a hive of bees, always buzzing, always crawling, and every so often stinging the shit out of him, he now walked wide to accommodate a massive case of blue balls.

It was the strangest thing, this obsessive fascination he had developed. He found himself trailing Willow when she wandered off, just to stay close. Whenever she muttered to herself, Sebastian strained to make out the words, just in case they were meant for him. And whenever she looked at him, he was a total goner.

Something was wrong here. Not that he didn't find Willow attractive—he did. Very much so. But he'd never had such a powerful, physical reaction before.

Would you have, though, with the curse riding your ass day and night?

Good point.

But even so, he felt like a pervert each time he went upstairs to use the bathing room, stopping by her bed along the way, just to smell her pillows. He hadn't known it was possible to jerk off ten times a day and still feel this unsatisfied. Sebastian had gotten more pleasure out of a wet dream about Willow than from the hollow act of making himself come. It couldn't be normal.

With a whirl of heavy skirts, the object of the most persistent sexual fantasy he'd ever had threw up her hands. "I can't stand this! I want to do something!"

I want to bend you over the table and throw your skirts up over your head. I want to be balls-deep in you again, because I somehow know exactly how amazing it'd feel and I crave it like a drug I never actually tasted. "Like what?"

"I don't know. *Something.*" She almost looked at him that time but caught herself before they made eye contact. Her cheeks blushed, and Sebastian couldn't get the dream image of her out of his head.

The buzzing in his bones worsened, the ache in his balls deepened all the way to his spine, but he still managed to keep the conversation going. "Helegert's a big place. We could keep exploring like we did yesterday." *When I dreamed about your thighs on either side of my head, and my tongue stuck in your pussy.* His mouth watered and Sebastian started feeling out of breath. She was right. Sitting here, doing nothing, would drive them both insane.

Willow was shaking her head. "Boring. I need outside." She turned toward the door, for all the world as if she would run straight out into the storm and for a second, her hair turned as pale as it'd been in his dream.

Sebastian had gotten an eyeful of her front then, but not her back. He didn't know how, but somehow he knew that those same strange blue tattoos that had flickered over her skin would have covered her back, too. He wanted to see that—*needed* to learn each one, and how it related to the others, and what they meant.

He grasped for logic. "If we go out there, we'll freeze."

"It's not that far to the summer garden. We could make it."

"And then we'll be just as stuck there as we are here." Without any walls or doors to put between them when things got out of control.

"But we'd be *outside.*" That time, she did meet his gaze, and her face momentarily went blank, her eyelids drooping sleepily. Before his eyes, her lips turned a brighter red, and Sebastian almost shot out of his seat to tackle her for a taste of them.

He'd kissed her once before, hadn't he? Sebastian vaguely recalled the feel of her soft lips as he made love to her mouth.

But not in last night's dream. Why hadn't he kissed her then? She'd asked him to; begged him, even.

And he'd almost done it, too, but at the last second, he'd pressed his mouth against her neck instead, tasting the cool salt of her skin rather than the enticing red of her lips, and it'd felt like he'd just dodged a trap.

What a crazy fucking dream!

At the opposite end of the table, Willow grasped the edge of the wood as if to stop herself from advancing. "How do you feel today?"

Like I'll die if I don't fuck you. "Almost back to normal." *If there even is such a thing for me anymore.*

Willow leaned over the table toward him. "Any pain?" She wasn't blinking.

Sebastian shook his head, shifting to meet her halfway. That dreamy, floating sensation came back, muting the buzzing in his bones as if all the bees suddenly decided to take flight at the same time, bringing him out of his chair and toward Willow.

He'd do it. He'd kiss her if it was the last thing he did. Sebastian barely breathed, staring at those lips, remembering—or imagining?—their taste. Like the sweetest winter fruits, always with a hint of frost…

The width of the table brought them up short, startling them both out of the odd trance. Willow blinked and looked away first, releasing Sebastian to resume breathing. This was ridiculous. "How about we go back to that underground room you showed me yesterday?"

"What for?"

Should he tell her? She hadn't responded the way he'd hoped when he'd offered to take her to Kesteran with him. He would have thought she'd jump at the chance to leave this frozen heap of rocks behind, but she seemed to genuinely like it here. Part of him argued that she didn't know any better, but Snow's warning about bad blood between the family branches kept him from pushing the issue prematurely.

Not to mention her offhand remark about any relatives not letting her live this way for so long. If he told her now that her cousin was the king of Valefort, she'd probably do the exact opposite of what he wanted.

Instead of opening up that hellish can of worms, he shrugged. "To snoop. That place is like a buried treasure chamber. Who knows what great stuff is hidden there?"

Willow shrugged. "Meh."

"What other options do we have for entertainment around here?" *I can think of a few…*

She must have heard the subliminal suggestion in his voice, because for a moment, she got that sleepy look in her eyes again and her hand fluttered up to the edge of her bodice, tugging it away from the wool undershirt as if she suddenly felt overheated.

He could help her. He knew how those laces tended to knot. He could untangle them for her; tug the bodice down her pale shoulders and lick across the delicate wings of her collarbones.

What he'd give to know her thoughts. To know whether she'd seen his dream last night, or shared it…

"Fine," Willow said, then shook her head, sending skeins of gray hair whipping around her face. She hadn't braided it today. He liked that. "Let's go digging through old, dusty junk in the dungeon."

Sebastian waved her to take the lead before he stood from the table. "After you, mistress."

Down into the dungeon they went, with Willow conjuring lights again to illuminate the spooky cavernous passageways. This place would never stop giving Sebastian the creeps. He constantly felt like something was watching him.

Luckily, in her current restless state, Willow dived right into the first trunk she came across. Expensive fabrics and small, precious metal odds and ends went flying as she dug down to the bottom, showing absolutely no care for those priceless antiques.

Sebastian watched the whirlwind of haphazard displacement for a moment to see if anything would catch her interest. She did hold up an ornate silver bottle for a moment, but when she opened it and found the contents to be perfume Sebastian could smell from several paces away, she made a face, closed the bottle and tossed it away before turning her attention to another trunk.

He could watch her for hours, thoroughly entranced with her smallest gestures.

He could also just as easily take a knee behind her, part her legs as she bent over the trunk, and feed his cock inside her inch by inch until she moaned his name in abandon.

But Sebastian still had a mission to complete: Bring Willow to Kesteran. And the first step to gaining her cooperation had to be finding out why her ancestor got disinherited and banished from Sturmgard in the first place. If any clues or accounts from that time still existed, this was the most likely place for them to be.

So he forced himself to turn his back on Willow and breathe down his rock-hard erection. *Remember your oath. Your life still belongs to Snow. You cannot fail her again.*

It worked.

By focusing on his duty, Sebastian was able to tune out the little humming noises Willow made as she muttered to herself and get to work sorting through the items on his side of the chamber.

Right off the bat, he found a scroll that had the royal seal of Sturmgard stamped into the wax on one corner, but that was about all that had survived. What little parchment remained attached to it—a strip less than a third of its original width—was faded and illegible.

Thinking he was on the right track, he dug through box after box of personal items but found nothing else of note. Just old jewelry and ancient underthings no one in their right mind would wear these days.

Moving on to the next box, he found it locked. "I'm assuming you have no sentimental attachment to this stuff?"

"None whatsoever."

Sebastian picked up one of the daggers and stabbed it into the lock's seam. A couple of good kicks and the lock fell apart. He pried open the lid. "Whoa…"

"What? Did you find something good?" In the next instant, Willow was plastered against his back where he knelt before the case, her face next to his and her hair obscuring his view.

His focused, detached brain short-circuited. The world went dark, and Sebastian became awash in the feel of her naked breasts pressing against his back, her hands roaming over his chest, down his stomach, to his cock. He imagined her lips against his spine as she brought him to the very edge of coming—

"Oh, look at that." She reached forward, her chest pressing against his shoulder, and picked up a heavy golden tome that looked like a creepy ancient spell book. Awash in her scent, the feel of her hair sliding like so much silk across his skin, Sebastian sucked in a harsh breath and curled his fingers into the edge of the trunk so hard the old wood creaked. And he couldn't move. If he did, he'd fall on Willow like a mindless animal, consequences be damned.

Fucking breathe!

He sucked air in and out of his lungs, pressed his raging hard-on against the trunk's engraved front panel to force it back under control. He thought up the night he'd almost died, but instead of dampening his need, the memory warped into a fantasy that stoked it even higher. He imagined Willow straddling him and riding him to release, her hair wild and her pale skin tattooed in strange blue designs. Even the paralyzing pain in that fantasy somehow became erotic, placing him at her mercy, and her pleasure.

Heedless of the massive tailspin she'd sent him into, Willow sat down next to him with her back to the box, flicked off the clasp with a fingertip, and opened the book, making its hinges squeak.

She became instantly absorbed in the writing, oblivious to Sebastian kneeling next to her, staring at her like a starving beast at a banquet. He wanted her to look at him the way she read that book; he craved all her attention, and her touch—everything. And he hated that book for taking Willow miles away from him, when she was sitting just there.

Remember your duty.

Sebastian squeezed his eyes shut and gritted his teeth. Willow was King Marcus' cousin. What the fuck was he doing even thinking about sex with her?

That almost restored his self-control to manageable levels.

And then she had to go and *ooohh* at something she'd read, sending him spinning right back to that dark, wild place he couldn't crawl out of, where all her sighs were for him, and all he had to go on was the feel of her body writhing against his, her legs clutching tightly around him, and her nails scratching down his back as he drove into her so deep he couldn't tell where he ended and she began.

Control yourself, Collins! Unlocking his jaw enough to speak, he asked, "What is it?"

It took Willow several seconds to answer. "Looks like a family history. Birth dates, death dates, wedding dates… The Ericksson royal line. Who are they?"

She has no idea… How could she not know anything about her own family? Had no one told her? Had they even known themselves? "How recent are those records?" *Yes, that's it. Focus on what you're here to do: bring King Marcus' cousin to Kesteran.*

Willow turned to the last marked page, less than halfway into the book. "The last entry is… It's…" She turned her wide eyes on him, her mouth agape.

Sebastian shifted to sit beside her so he could read for himself. "Sindrea Faithblade. Died ten years ago at the age of thirty-six."

"My…" Willow swallowed with a gulp louder than her voice. "My mother."

Thirty-six. She'd died so young. "My grandmother must have recorded this." Willow had been ten years old at the time of her mother's death. She remembered little of her when she'd been alive, but the day she'd died was still fresh in her mind. "Rowena said my mother died of loneliness. And that *she* would die of a broken heart. She did, too. About two years after we burned my mother's body."

"I'm sorry," Sebastian said. "How old were you?"

"Twelve. I couldn't move Rowena from her bed, so I had to use magic. My first time casting a spell all on my own."

"You had to do it on your own?"

"There was no one else around."

"And you've lived here all alone since then?" There was an angry sort of awe in his voice when he demanded. "Why?"

Willow sighed. "I already told you. Helegert is my home. It's where I belong."

After a pause, Sebastian took the tome from her and spread it over both their laps. Flipping the pages back, he pointed to an entry. "Look at this. The date is smudged, but it looks like Alvina Ericksson was the first to change her name. She became Alvina of the Issaven."

Willow frowned. Why did that sound familiar?

"She must have done it again later and never recorded it. Her daughter was born Elena Faithblade."

Willow touched the page, her fingers gently skimming the elegant, slanted script. Someone must have taken great care to record these things—in the beginning. But as time went on, the script changed. The lines became unevenly spaced, the lettering more haphazard, as if some noble tradition of recordkeeping had become an unwanted burden.

Tearing her gaze away, she glanced back at the open chest. "Are there more of these?"

For the next several hours, the two of them scoured hundreds of pages of royal records, personal correspondences, and private journals. Willow became entranced by what they uncovered. Suddenly, she had a history—a royal one! And that amazing, but abstract idea soon became so personal, she hunched over private journals, as if those secret thoughts could still cause the writer great harm.

She read the heartless royal decree that had banished Alvina Ericksson—not just one of the royal house, but a princess second in line for the throne—from Sturmgard. The king and queen had magnanimously allowed her to take what should have been her dowry into exile, and there was an itemized list of everything she'd been given.

No personal keepsakes, no favorite paintings, or blankets, or pets. Only a wardrobe fashioned of the finest materials, a chest of jewels to befit a princess, gold coins for her coffers, and what amounted to a Sturmgard propaganda kit of banners, royal seals, and the like.

They'd disinherited her, had taken their name from her but had furnished her with a treasure trove of items to forever remind her of what she'd lost.

How utterly cruel.

In a smaller, ornately engraved wooden box, Willow found letters Alvina had written to her parents and siblings from exile, all of which had been returned unopened. She'd written about her new home, and the love of her life, and the beautiful daughter she'd born him.

But her pain, loneliness, and heartbreak, she'd saved for her private journals, never to be shared with anyone, not even the mysterious man who'd eventually abandoned her as well.

Willow found Elena's journals, too. And her daughter's, and hers. Four generations of daughters born out of wedlock, the older teaching the younger lessons of bitterness, mistrust, and isolation. With each word she read, Willow saw Alvina's heartbreak bleeding down through her descendants, at first poisoning them against the Ericksson line, and then deliberately locking away any knowledge of them altogether, until they'd become forgotten.

Helegert is our home now, a passage read. *It is our refuge and our responsibility. Nothing else matters, but what happens within its walls. Nothing else exists, but what we choose to create right here. Take care of the keep, my dear, and it will forever take care of you.*

"Willow?"

"Hmm?"

"Did you hear what I said?"

She shook herself, took off her spectacles to rub her tired eyes. "No, sorry. What was it?" It had to be nearing night. Now that her concentration had been disrupted, Willow began to feel the gnaw of hunger. Her mouth was parched, and her lower half had gone numb from sitting on the hard stone floor.

Sebastian looked in no better shape. His hair looked like he'd spent the last hour tugging on it, and when he stood, he winced. "I said I think I found the reason why Alvina was exiled."

"Oh?" Willow pushed to her feet and immediately lost her balance. With a squeak, she listed to the side, flailing to catch herself. Luckily, Sebastian had excellent reflexes. He dropped the journal he was holding and lunged forward, catching her against him.

Stuck together from chest to knee, their noses brushing, they froze, gazes locked. Willow forgot to breathe. Her fingers curled into his shoulders as dizziness assailed her, and she could have sworn she heard faint strains of a waltz from somewhere far away. "I…"

"Yes," Sebastian whispered, his arms tightening around her to lift her up a little more.

Willow needed to feel his skin against hers, the way she had in her dream. She craved the wild passion they'd shared, instinctively knowing the dream version had been the merest hint of what they could have together, and her body eagerly responded. It went beyond physical desire, far beyond even the relentless urges the bond between them brought up. Willow yearned for Sebastian with a fierceness that frightened her. In that moment, she would have given him anything—*anything*—for one taste of his lips. Just thinking about it gave her that same lightheaded sense of hot and cold, but *right*. And so very *good*.

I could spend eternity right here.

Sebastian broke eye contact when he thumped his forehead to hers. "We should go back upstairs," he said, his voice whispering across her lips, straight to her abdomen. Her knees, already weakened, buckled completely, but the way Sebastian held her, he barely seemed to notice.

She heard his stomach rumble, and hers answered in kind. Willow managed a wry grin and, though he couldn't see it with his eyes closed, he reciprocated. "I suppose you're right," she relented, but made no move to remove herself from his embrace.

Just one kiss…

With a sigh, Sebastian set her away, peeling her from his body slowly, and making a face as if it caused him physical pain. "What time do you suppose it is?"

"Late," was all she could say. "Pain?"

He shook his head, but she could tell he was lying. What she couldn't tell was whether it was from their time down here, or still the remnants of Zorana's curse.

Or the new effects of mine…

"I'll get you more of that potion." It took a tremendous effort to turn away from him, like tearing two magnets apart. But once she faced the door, it became easier to keep going.

"What for?" he said, following close at her heels. "It doesn't seem to do much."

"But it does do something. Maybe I just got the dosage wrong." Quite possible. But it was also possible that the potion did absolutely nothing at all. Still, at least it made *her* feel better. She was doing *something* to try to fix this mess.

Upstairs, the fire had gone out, and the kitchen was freezing. The storm seemed to have eased, but now there was a glistening border of ice around the edges of the door and window shutters. She'd have to use magic to get them open again.

Sebastian layered the kindling and sparked a flame. Willow fed it more wood and magic, building the fire up quickly so they could warm themselves.

"How long do these storms usually last?"

Willow shrugged. "In the winter, they're almost constant. I had planned to build a walkway from the kitchen to the summer garden this year, a tunnel of sorts to keep out the elements, but I haven't gotten around to it yet."

"At this rate, we'll run out of wood by tomorrow."

"There's more in the old pantry. And the bedroom doesn't need any…" The log she held fell out of her grasp as she pictured herself pressed against the heat of his body in her bed upstairs. She imagined his hands roaming over her back; his mouth trailing across her chest—

The tether gave a hard jerk, demanding she go to Sebastian, take off his clothes, and her own, and share body heat between them. It didn't scream; it whispered insistently how she should touch him, and have him touch her. That she should kiss him to relieve the throbbing ache in her lips.

That it would all be so much better, so much sweeter even than her dream—because it'd be real.

The relentless command was so powerful, her feet turned her halfway toward him, and her ears became deaf to everything besides her own breath. Sebastian was talking, but she didn't register his words, only the timbre of his voice humming through her body, making her feel dreamy and languid.

When she found herself nearing him, she forced her feet to change direction and go to the cupboard instead. Shaking, Willow filled a cup with her potion, then picked it up with both hands and brought it to Sebastian, staring at the contents so she wouldn't be tempted to look at him. "Have a drink."

"You really think it'll do any good?" Had his voice turned husky? It felt like it.

Willow exhaled on a shiver and, raising her gaze to his chin, but no higher, she said, "Humor me."

He didn't move right away. Willow sensed he was studying her, that he wanted to say something, but in the end, he merely raised the cup and downed its contents in two swallows. "Anything to please you," he joked. Did he realize how eerily it rang with truth?

"Thank you," she said, reclaiming the now empty cup. Only then did she trust herself to meet his gaze and smile. And as she did, the pinched look on his face smoothed out, and he smiled back, albeit crookedly.

Kiss…

Willow couldn't tear her gaze away. They were standing too close again, her skirts brushing around his legs. She could almost feel how chilled he was, but with each passing second, his skin pinkened a little more as the fire warmed them both. Willow wanted to taste him. She hadn't gotten a chance in her dream last night, and it felt like a grievous omission she needed to rectify.

Now.

Kiiiissssss…

THUD. THUD. THUD.

"What was that?"

"The front door," she answered, thinking of his lips massaging hers, their tongues twining together, and breaths mingling… Then her eyes shot wide. "The front door!"

CHAPTER 11

W illow, wait!" Sebastian ran after her as she raced for the front door. For wearing at least a dozen pounds of skirts, she was surprisingly swift on her feet. "Slow down, will you?"

She didn't. He caught up with her as she was sticking her arm out through the hole in the wall by the front door to clear away some of the snow. Dull light shone in through the small opening she'd made, indicating early morning. They'd spent the whole day and night down in that dungeon. No wonder he was so hungry.

With a frustrated growl, Willow retreated back inside. "Can't see anything. Help me with this, will you?"

Sebastian grabbed hold of the massive door handle above and below her hands, braced his foot on the other side, and pulled as hard as he could, but the door was frozen solid and had been for a very long time. "Isn't there another way out?"

"Through the kitchen. Do you want to walk that in the storm?"

"Then we'll just wait it out." He leaned into the hole where snow had already covered the opening Willow had made and shouted, "Come back when the storm passes!" Unlikely whoever was on the other side could hear him.

Willow gasped. "That could take days!"

THUD. THUD. THUD.

Nope. Definitely hadn't heard.

"Whoever it is wouldn't have come unless it was important," Willow insisted, taking hold of the handle again. "We need to get this door open now."

She did have a point. And, having been on the other side of that door recently, he felt a twinge of guilty compassion for the visitor with ridiculously bad timing. Shaking out his cold hands, he braced himself again and redoubled his efforts, pulling with all his might.

Nothing. Not even a groan or a crack to indicate they'd made any difference whatsoever.

THUD. THUD. THUD.

Sebastian let go. "It's not working. You'll have to use magic to thaw it some. We'll never get it open this way."

She huffed unhappily and released her death grip to massage her hands. They were red and probably cramped from her efforts. He was reaching out to take over for her when her words pulled him up short. "I was hoping I wouldn't have to do this."

"Why? Seems like the easiest solution."

"Because magic sometimes has…unintended consequences."

A red flag of warning briefly flashed in his mind at the way her voice had cracked at that last bit, but he brushed it off. "What kind of consequences?" And shouldn't she be immune to them?

She hitched a shoulder in an uneasy shrug, studying the door. "Well, I'll need heat to melt the snow and ice, so…"

"So it'll probably be heat that blows back up in our faces. Well, lucky this place is made of stone. Not much left to burn here."

Willow gave him an odd look. "Not that kind of heat." She didn't drop her gaze the way she usually did, and the buzzing that had momentarily eased after he'd drunk her potion in the kitchen redoubled, making his entire body tense and quiver. "I can absorb it, but you…"

In other words, if she thawed that door, she'd be risking him spiraling out of control. And that was a very short trip for him as it was. Would he even retain any semblance of higher thought once she started working her spell? "I could go upstairs." Maybe if he was far enough, he wouldn't be affected—

Willow shook her head. "No, I need you here to open the door once it's thawed enough."

No way. It was too risky. They should let whoever was out there take the hint and come back another time. And that logic would have been so much more effective if she hadn't been staring at him so intently, waiting for him to make the choice.

Somehow, in that moment, against all common sense, Sebastian knew her thoughts as clearly as his own. He felt her body respond to the idea, and it wasn't with fear. Even from several steps away, he could almost feel her breath against his skin and hear her heart racing. She never blinked or looked away, and in her eyes, he glimpsed the same hunger that rode him without mercy.

Yet she fought her own desire to let him decide. Both of them knew that once she started, whatever was done would never be undone. And she still willingly gave all the power of that choice to him.

So Sebastian gave it right back to her. "Your call." The words came out with difficulty, and he couldn't expand on the sentiment if he'd tried. Not with his blood burning so much for the feel of her cool skin he started sweating in the icy entry hall—and Willow hadn't even begun her spell yet. *Want me,* he silently willed. *Need me as much as I need you.*

Willow shivered, as if she'd heard him and an explosive sigh started Sebastian breathing again when she squared her shoulders and rubbed her hands together, warning, "Stay behind me."

Sebastian positioned himself at her back, giving her enough room to move. He sensed the powers swirl around her as she began, drawing up heat from the ground and giving it direction and focus.

Almost instantly, Sebastian felt its effects on him. A dream-like haze washed over him, making sight and sound softer. His breathing became labored, his body swayed toward Willow, and almost involuntarily, he began tugging his shirt loose. Her hair billowed up in the warm air currents, exposing her wool undershirt where it gaped in the back and bared her pale nape and shoulders. The hot wind teased him with her sweet scent, lured him to the spot where her neck met her shoulder; where he could see the faintest of blue lines begin to bloom out from her spine along the surface of her skin.

Willow performed an intricate ballet of hand movements, feeding that heat forward in an even flow, and Sebastian could tell exactly how the magic moved through her, and beyond her. It lovingly traced the curves of her body, snaking up around her legs, seeping in through her torso, up to her chest, and there it gained strength, swirling madly as it fought her control, tried to burst out all at once. Willow's focus was the only thing keeping it in check; keeping it from overtaking her and exploding the front door altogether.

When she swayed, Sebastian stepped up, pulled her back against his chest, shuddering at how good it felt just to hold her. He could feel the erratic beat of her heart against his forearm, the immense heat passing through her like water through an ice sculpture. Despite the magic she channeled—or because of it?—her body remained cool to the touch.

Sebastian brushed aside her wild gray mane, put his mouth to the spot that called to him so sweetly, and licked. He felt her shiver as her focus slipped, a burst of heat breaking away from her and slamming into the door, turning it momentarily red hot. Another such burst and it would shatter.

But she was already finished, leashing the magic back in through herself, back into the ground. It passed through him as well, and he held Willow tighter, pressed his heated cheek against hers to somehow cool this fever wracking him from head to toe.

Blood thrumming through his veins so loud he could hear it, sight focused on the blue swirls on Willow's skin, Sebastian lost all awareness of the outside world as Willow turned in his arms and pulled his shirt off over his head. Before he could even reach for the lacing on her dress, it dropped away from her, and then she was in his arms again, her bare chest pressed against his, her legs around his waist.

In a flash, he had her pressed against the warmed wooden door, and he was rocking against her, reveling in the breathy sounds she made at his ear, the way her nails dug into his shoulders, telling him she needed more.

He did, too.

With all the dexterity of a hormonal teenager, he ripped open his fly. At his cock's first contact with her, Willow gave a lusty shout, rocking into him, clawing at him. Sebastian was already at the very precipice; one wrong move and he'd go off like a fireworks display.

Not before she gets there first.

He grabbed onto her hips, shoved them back against the wall harder than he'd intended, but she didn't seem to mind. Holding her still, Sebastian reached between them, spread the lips of her sex, and rubbed into the wetness there, from the tip of her clit, to the bottom edge of her pussy, and back again, over and over, until his hand was drenched and Willow was keening for release.

Only then did he feed his cock into her. Breath left him in a baffled, *Whuh!* As he slid as deep as her body would allow. Gooseflesh prickled all over his skin at the feel of her wet, cool sheath gloving him, squeezing him. He'd never felt anything like it.

And he never wanted to leave.

Willow was out of her head with lust, fighting for breath, clawing at Sebastian, loving the way he filled her with heat and power—but why wouldn't he move?

She arched against him, rubbed her aching nipples across his hard chest. His muscles twitched everywhere they touched, and it was because of her; because of the effect she had on him. That knowledge filled her with a confidence she hadn't felt before, and a terrible need to somehow…somehow…

He pulled back and thrust up, bouncing her against the door.

"Sebastian!"

He did it again, his fingers flexing and curling into the flesh of her behind in an odd sort of massage that heightened the sensations below her waist. She curled her hips to meet his next thrust, making him groan.

Better than my dream.

So much more than any dream possibly could be.

The door at her back cooled, the wind howled beyond it, blowing in puffs of snow through the hole right next to her like butterfly kisses over her shoulder. The snowflakes touched down over her arm but didn't melt.

Sebastian adjusted his grip, altered his angle a little, and pumped into her hard and fast, making her body hum with something akin to joy. The pleasure built, and built, and built some more, and still, Willow couldn't quite seem to reach the pinnacle.

Feeling Sebastian's eyes on her, she met his gaze and saw the raw hunger burning in their depths. He missed nothing—savored the sounds she made, devoured the squeeze of her thighs around him, the rake of her nails across his back. He seemed to feed on the smallest of reactions and use them to drive her absolutely and utterly *mad*.

"Please," she gasped, bouncing up and down as his hips slapped against her flesh. "Please, Sebastian, pleasepleaseplease…"

Sebastian groaned, adjusted his grip and reached between them once more. The instant he touched her, Willow went off, screaming his name. He kept the pleasure rolling, with his thumb firmly against her clit as he continued to rock against her.

And then he pulled out with a harsh curse, thrusting against her abdomen as he spent, and Willow felt his pleasure as if it were her own. It set her off a second time, made her bury her mouth against his shoulder to hold in another scream.

Sebastian pulled her away from the door, sat down with her in his lap, holding her close as they both caught their breaths.

"Consequences," she purred and, utterly spent, promptly fell asleep.

Sebastian shifting position woke her up sometime later. "Sorry," he said, wincing. "Didn't mean to wake you. Was getting a little chilly."

"No, s'alright." Willow straightened her glasses and stood up from Sebastian's lap, then helped him get back to his feet. He groaned, shaking feeling back into his legs, and Willow flushed with guilt. "I'm sorry."

He frowned at her. "For what?"

Willow gestured around them with an awkward wave of her arm.

"For this. If you hadn't been coerced by the magic, you wouldn't have—"

Sebastian covered her mouth with a gentle hand. "Don't assume you know what I would or wouldn't have done." He looked almost angry, but his hands on her were so gentle. "You can't deny we've been circling each other for days. This would have happened eventually, with or without magic. And I'm not letting you take it back."

Willow wanted so badly to believe him, but now that her mind was clear she knew better. And perhaps he did, too. Maybe that was why he said all those things as if he was trying to convince himself as much as her. She shifted her gaze to his chest and felt a sharp pang to discover that nothing had changed between them. That tether still bound them with magical fibers Sebastian would never see, and might never even be aware of. Satisfied for the moment, its relentless pull had lessened but hadn't disappeared.

And Willow felt like the lowest kind of vermin for not telling him the truth.

"Besides, that was the best time I ever had in bed," he said with an easy half-grin, stabbing her with another dagger of guilt. "Or, you know. Whatever."

The wind wailed another gust outside, bringing in a shower of snowflakes through the hole by the door. Gods this storm had no end in sight!

Then she remembered why they'd come out here in the first place and gasped, diving for her clothes. She pulled everything on over her head, not bothering with the laces, and grasped the door handle again, yanking hard.

The portal gave a groan and a crack and budged open a few inches, enough for her to see there was no one waiting outside. Disappointed, she began to close it again when a flutter of movement caught her eye. Someone had pinned a letter to the door with a thin, sharp dagger.

Willow retrieved both before she closed the door again.

Sebastian, fully dressed now, breathed into his hands for warmth as he came up behind her. "You got mail."

He stood so close, she'd only have to lean back to touch him. She almost did, too, languid with a comfort and familiarity she had no right to feel. Doing her best to ignore it, she headed back to the kitchen, where the fire had probably gone out yet again. "It appears so." The dagger was small and plain, no marks on it to identify the owner or maker. The envelope, too, only had Willow's full name on it.

Sebastian got right to work on the fire. "Well, open it."

She did, and read over the handful of sentences three times, smiling bigger and bigger with each read. "The mayor of Icerton wrote on behalf of the town. It says the storm froze their crops and they're 'open to negotiation.' Do you know what this means?"

"Uh, no, not really."

Willow squealed and twirled around the kitchen with utter glee. "It means they're desperate enough to trade now. Means they want to buy produce from my summer garden. And look, they even addressed it to Willow Faithblade, lady of Helegert Keep."

"As opposed to…?"

"Ghoul, witch, the gray-haired freak—"

He held up a hand. "So how much will you charge them?"

Willow frowned. "What do you mean?"

Sebastian looked at her as if she'd sprouted another head. "You control the only food supply for miles. You could make a fortune."

"You want me to extort starving people for profit?"

"They called you names—to your face. They shunned you and ignored you, and gods know what else. Why the hell *wouldn't* you?"

"Oh, I don't care about any of that. What matters is the lines of communication are now open—"

"Yeah, for how long?"

"—I can fix everything now that they're willing to talk."

He sighed. "Willow, these people didn't give two shits about you your entire life, and they're not going to start now."

She scowled at him, then headed out into the storage closet where she'd left her snow gear. "I'm not going to let them starve if that's what you're hoping for."

"I'm not saying you should," he said, following behind, taking the snow beast fur clothes from her so she could put on long underpants under her skirts and strip off her dress to replace it with a thinner wool shirt. "I'm just saying don't get your hopes up too high. Don't give away the farm."

Funny, that was exactly what she'd been wanting to do since she'd created it. Willow *wanted* the people of Icerton to take ownership of it. She *wanted* them to want that produce because that meant they'd come to Helegert to farm the land for themselves, and that meant she wouldn't be alone here anymore.

Willow tied her hair back, then thrust her legs one at a time into the fur pants Sebastian held for her and muttered a barely coherent, "Thanks."

"It won't change anything," he continued, helping her loop the straps over her shoulders. "It won't make them suddenly like you."

"You don't know that," she insisted, stuffing her arms through the fur jacket sleeves when he held it out to her.

"Believe me," he said, catching the edges closed to button the coat. "I know. People don't change. They may pretend until they get what they want, but deep down, an asshole will always be an asshole, and sooner or later, you will get crushed by the weight of all his shit." Done with the buttons, he pulled the hood up over her head.

Willow sighed. She knew he was right. If the people of Icerton hadn't warmed up to her by now, they never would. Maybe the best solution really was to negotiate a fair price.

But what in the world would she do with the money? She already had two cellars full of gold coins and nothing to spend them on, since no one would trade with her.

"You want to see something funny?"

Sebastian rolled his eyes. "Sure."

Willow tugged the hood down lower over her forehead, closed the collar all the way up over her nose, and then let out a deep breath that fogged up her glasses. She giggled, amused as always, which made her glasses fog up more.

When they finally cleared, she found Sebastian grinning and shaking his head. "Yours is a happy nature, sweet one." He reached out as if to cup her cheek under the hood, then seemed to reconsider. "Go do whatever it is you're going to do. I'll keep the fire going in here."

Willow nodded as much as her heavy clothing would allow, then waddled out through the kitchen door, which promptly closed behind her to keep out the wind.

The best thing about the snow beast suit, aside from the fact that it kept her warm in any weather without making her sweat, was its added weight. It grounded her against the winds, kept her moving forward as she followed the invisible path to her summer garden.

Only there was no hint of green ahead to mark her destination, and when she reached the stone archway that should have been her sanctuary from the cold, Willow swayed, tripping back a step.

Her summer garden was…*gone*.

A thick glaze of ice covered the ground, gloving vines and branches, encasing fruits and leaves, locking it all into place. Drifts of snow arched left and right where she'd piled buckets, baskets, and tools. Her stone water well had a geyser spray jutting out of it, forever frozen in a glittering ice monument, like a centerpiece to the wholesale destruction of everything she'd spent years working for.

The only thing that had remained untouched was Sebastian's horse, huddling terrified in one corner where a trough of hay had been left for him.

Willow couldn't feel her hands or feet. She breathed so hard her glasses fogged over, and she had to wipe them off to see anything. How could this have happened? Her spells had been immaculate—they still were. She felt them in every stone making up the wall, and in the ground itself, sinking a dozen feet down. They *couldn't* have failed—

The storm died down with a suddenness that left her reeling, and in the ensuing silence, a rattling sound like ice shards clanging together drew her gaze to the north. There, at the top of the hill, stood the ice fey's chieftain, battle staff in hand, and teeth bared in a challenging snarl. Their gazes met over a mile of distance, and he thumped his staff down once, raising a flurry that spun up from the ground around him.

Willow shuddered at that display.

As if he'd sensed it, the ice fey hiss-screamed to the sky, and disappeared, his message delivered and received with painful clarity.

CHAPTER 12

To the Most Honorable Mayor Dahl and the Citizens of Icerton:

I deeply regret to inform you that, due to the unreasonable temper of the Ice Fey clan north of Helegert, I am no longer able to provide the town with produce from my summer garden, as it has been encased most thoroughly in ice. I am deeply sorry for this turn of events, which came about through no fault of my own. I had hoped a trade agreement between Helegert and Icerton could be negotiated to the benefit of both and very much looked forward to the dialogue.

As I now find myself in quite the bind as well, the only recourse left to me is to travel south to Kesteran, and petition Queen Snow White (who I have only recently been told is married to a cousin of mine—how odd is that?) for aid for Icerton and Helegert in their time of need.

*I understand the situation is already quite dire in Icerton, so I am leaving the doors of Helegert Keep wide open for your use. Within its walls are stored vast riches (which should allow you to procure plentiful supplies from other sources), and a terrible curse.**

It is my deepest hope, and fondest wish that I should be able to return to Helegert anon, with aid from the crown and the resources to restore my summer garden to its original state. Until then, I bid you all good fortune and offer prayers for your continued well-being.

With sincerest regards,
Lady Willow Faithblade of Helegert Keep

**The curse is not because of you! I simply had no place else to put it. Still and all, I would advise great caution while searching the lowest levels of the keep, as it has somewhat of a mind of its own and tends to move about unpredictably. But I am almost certain it cannot escape the binding I placed on it, so all should be well. I think.*

Mayor Dahl set the letter down next to his returned dagger and gaped at the assistant who had retrieved it from the front door. "She has gone utterly mad, Erol. My gods… We're doomed."

With two cases of Zorana-era gold coins, two more of old books and letters, and one trunk filled with their few belongings all stacked inside the carriage, there was nowhere for Sebastian and Willow to sit except in the front driver's seat. At least the weather had improved. Clear skies and bright sunshine made their departure as smooth as it could be, with Sebastian's one remaining horse struggling along the path.

Willow wasn't taking the trip very well. She wouldn't stop leaning over the side of the carriage to look behind them, and he was half afraid she'd jump off and run back to Helegert on foot. With each mile they gained, Willow became more and more agitated, nearing panic mode as they left White Plains behind and the endless stretches of bright white snow gave way to brown dirt and vibrant greenery. It was making *him* twitchy.

"You haven't asked me about Alvina yet," he said to distract her.

Without bothering to face him, she replied, "What about her?"

"About why she got sent into exile."

Willow shrugged.

Undaunted by her lack of interest, he kept talking. "She reneged on an arranged marriage to a prominent courtier. The day of their official betrothal, Alvina stood up before a throne room filled with nobles and visiting royalty and announced that she was pregnant with another man's child."

That seemed to catch Willow's interest enough for her to face him. "Are you joking?"

"Not at all. It's no wonder they went to such lengths to cover it up. Back in the day, breaking an arranged royal marriage was tantamount to treason. Her intended was so insulted he threatened war against the crown and, at that point, her parents really had no other choice. Exile was the most lenient punishment they could have delivered without plunging Sturmgard into a civil war. The interesting thing is the decree didn't specify Helegert as her place of exile; it seems Alvina chose it for herself." Although he had no idea why.

"Who was the child's father?"

Sebastian shrugged. "Under penalty of death, she refused to divulge his name. I was hoping she might have mentioned it in her private journals somewhere. That's why I wanted to bring them with us."

"The new name she took might be a clue."

Sebastian shifted in his seat to find a more comfortable position. His bones were starting to hum again. A far cry from the wretched agony he'd endured before Willow's healing, but still persistent enough to make him worry something had gone wrong with her spell. "Might. Might not." When they reached Kesteran, he'd get Declan to take a proper look at him. A second opinion couldn't hurt. "Based on the dates, she took the name a month after she arrived in White Plains. We can't assume that her lover followed her into exile. Especially since there would have been a price on his head in Sturmgard."

"Well, why not, if he loved her?"

"Sturmgard had an ice cold policy on treason," he replied tugging the reins to steer the horse farther around a puddle that looked too much like a sinkhole for his peace of mind. The last thing they needed now was to get stuck in the middle of nowhere, still outside of signal range. "Whether or not he'd remained in Sturmgard, they would have retaliated without mercy. Against him, or his family. He wouldn't have risked that by officially marrying Alvina and revealing his name."

"Not even for love? Not even for his own child?" Her outrage practically called him a heartless monster. Willow had no idea of the consequences of going against a powerful, magically gifted monarch.

Sebastian hated having to be the one to enlighten her. "If it meant his brothers, sisters, and their children were made to suffer for it? Would *you* have done it?"

The way she dropped her gaze said no, she wouldn't have. He could practically feel how ashamed she was of her own, hypothetical decision.

"Don't feel bad. It would have been an impossible choice either way. Alvina was no fool herself; she knew what she was doing when she made her announcement. My guess is that she resented having her husband chosen for her and did the only thing she could to get out of it."

"She believed in love," Willow murmured. "And love failed her."

"How so?"

With a shrug, she looked off to the side again, speaking to the land rather than him. "One of her early journals said her lover left before she gave birth to Elena. That must have been why she changed her name a second time. I think he did follow her to Valefort. And I think they did get married, and something happened to make him abandon her."

"Did she mention his name?"

Willow shook her head. "Alvina only referred to him as 'my beloved.'" She met his gaze to add, "Even after he left her. Until her last day, she only ever referred to him as 'my beloved.' She didn't sleep with him to get out of an arranged marriage. She did it because she loved him."

Sebastian gave a cautious nod. "I believe you." Even if he didn't believe the man had loved Alvina back. If he had, he never would have abandoned his pregnant wife in a shithole like Helegert. In Sebastian's book, that made the man, whoever he'd been, the worst kind of bastard.

Willow huffed, wriggling in her seat and tugging on her gown. "How much farther is it to Kesteran?"

They were heading toward much warmer climes; she had to be overheating in those thick layers. Sebastian himself was feeling warm, and he wasn't wearing ten pounds of wool. "We're only going as far as Oberland today. Once we get within signal range, I can call ahead and reserve a hotel room for the night. We'll rest up, and tomorrow I'll have a proper car waiting for us. It'll be a much faster ride the rest of the way to Kesteran." Not to mention more comfortable. "Can you hold on a few more hours?"

With angry jerks, Willow tugged the laces completely free of her gown's bodice, then pulled the whole thing off over her head and tossed it to the ground. Left in nothing but a worn, crumpled under gown that reached to mid-calf and teased the shadows of her dusky nipples, she sat back and breathed a big sigh. "Now I can."

Sebastian bit down on the inside of his cheek until he tasted blood, but the pain had absolutely no effect on his hardon.

It was going to be a long, long drive…

They didn't reach the Grand Hotel Oberland until well after nightfall. An attendant ran out as soon as they stopped in front of the hotel to take over the care of their horse and carriage, and two more came to remove their luggage into the lobby. "Leave it all," Sebastian told them. "But make sure it's secure. All we need is the topmost trunk."

"Yes, sir," the head attendant replied, politely averting his gaze from Willow, and she belatedly remembered she was still in her chemise.

Crossing her arms over her chest, she hunched in on herself and shifted half behind Sebastian as the attendant added, "If you please, sir, your room has been prepared. The concierge has your keys ready at the front desk."

The smallest flicker of the man's gaze to Willow brought her to Sebastian's attention. Looking as exhausted as she felt, he took off his jacket and draped it over her before wordlessly leading her into the lobby.

As beautiful as the building was on the outside, on the inside, the splendor was almost too much to take in. A rich, red carpet ran the length of the lobby from the outer staircase to the concierge desk. Electric sconces and chandeliers filled the chamber with light as bright as day, illuminating great big paintings in gilded frames.

Willow had never seen so much finery in all her life.

She was still gaping at the fancy modern television screens built *into* the walls when Sebastian took her hand to lead her away. A short ride in a claustrophobic little elevator later, they were walking down a hallway lined with portrait replicas to a door that opened as soon as Sebastian touched a little plastic square to a nondescript pad on the wall.

He ushered her in, tugged off his boots and threw himself back onto one of the big, plush beds with a heartfelt sigh that reminded her of how tired and sore she was. "Civilization. How I've missed thee!"

Scowling, Willow kicked at his dangling foot as she made her way around his bed to her own. She sat on it, sank down into several inches of plush pillow padding, and had to admit, at least to herself, that there was something to be said for creature comforts. "How much does it cost to spend a night in this place?"

Sebastian tilted his head back to look at her upside down. "Less than you think. The Royal Inn was all booked up for the night. This is the more modest alternative."

Willow could scarcely fathom that. What on earth kind of a lifestyle did the man have in Kesteran? No wonder he'd been so put out over Helegert's lack of…everything.

"But don't worry about cost. Queen Snow is picking up the tab for this."

"Why would she do that?"

Sebastian shrugged, then levered himself up to rub his lower back. "She wants to make a good impression. You are her husband's long lost cousin, after all."

Yes, so she'd been told. And despite now knowing on an intellectual level that King Marcus and his entire family owed her absolutely nothing after Alvina's betrayal, in her heart she still felt like an orphan who was somehow supposed to be grateful to have found adoptive relatives.

She'd barely gone halfway between the only home she'd ever known and her cousin's castle, and already she felt completely out of place. All this luxury and modern conveniences… Willow didn't know what to do with herself here.

Her lack of a verbal response made Sebastian sigh. "Come on, let me show you something."

Willow barely bit back a groan. "I'm really not in the mood for a walk."

"Then you're going to love this," he assured her with a grin, already tugging her to her feet. Through an unadorned wooden door, he led her into the bathing room. He turned a couple of knobs and within moments the chamber filled with steam as the bathtub filled up. Sebastian waggled his eyebrows at her. "You know you want to."

Sweet merciful gods, but she wanted to. Just the idea of a hot bath had her practically tearing off her under gown, and she almost fell over trying to tug her boots off. To his credit, Sebastian didn't laugh at her. In fact, he got really tense and quiet as she tossed away the last sock and heedlessly brushed past him to get into the tub.

Sebastian cleared this throat, staring at her discarded clothes. "I'll leave you to it."

"Stay," she said without thinking, then amended, "Please."

He turned to face her, but instead of meeting her gaze, he frowned at the edge of the tub. "I… That is… *Ahem.*"

"Are you all right?"

"We never talked about that spell of yours backfiring on us."

Willow blanched. A massive chill ran down her spine, and suddenly her steaming bath felt a whole lot cooler.

"Don't get me wrong, I enjoyed the hell out of it—*you*—I mean *it*. Dammit, I'm saying this all wrong."

"*Oh*, you're talking about the sex."

"Yes, I'm talking about the sex. What else would I be talking about?"

Grateful for the steam that disguised her guilty flush, Willow shrugged a shoulder. "I honestly haven't thought about it."

In a curious feat of coordinated multitasking, Sebastian somehow managed to scowl and roll his eyes at the same time. "Thanks a lot."

"What? I mean talking about it. I haven't thought about discussing it with you. I didn't realize we were supposed to. The sex was great. But I figured you wouldn't want to do it again since you told me you don't *want* to since the curse—"

"Oh, I want to."

Whatever else she might have said wafted away on a puff of steam as their tether tightened with an almost audible *snap* and her mind went blank. "You do?"

"I see you completely engulfed in a mountain of wool and snow beast coat and all I can think about is peeling it all off you layer by layer."

It's the spell talking. He doesn't know what he's saying.

"I watch you twirl around the kitchen, and it pisses me off that I can't pull you down on my lap and kiss you breathless."

Willow gripped the edge of the tub, her breathing becoming labored.

Sebastian noticed. A hot spark bloomed in his gaze as he stared at her knuckles and a healthy bulge tented the front of his pants. "You look away from me, and all I can do is wrack my brains for some way to make you look back. I want you so much it makes my bones hum, and that scares the shit out of me. So if you don't want me, if you're indifferent, tell me now. Make me leave. For fuck's sake, just put me out of my misery already."

CHAPTER 13

A small tsunami of warm water splashed Sebastian a second before Willow's slender body slammed into him. Sebastian slipped on the wet floor but managed to correct enough to catch himself on the vanity. Her arms and legs came around him, cooling so rapidly it made him shiver. He turned them around, planted her bare ass on the vanity, and leaned her back enough to get his hands between them. *Fuck*, the zipper on his drenched pants stuck.

While he wrestled with that, Willow's nimble fingers worked down the buttons of his shirt. She finished first, forcing him to give up his frustrated efforts to shrug the thing off, but his hands got stuck inside the sleeves, and when he tried to reach for her, those sleeves turned inside out. Sebastian growled, and Willow shivered, smiling in response.

A flash of blue caught his eye, but by the time he focused on the fogged-up mirror behind her, whatever he'd seen in the reflection of her back was gone. A frown knotted his brow. *What are you?*

Willow's hand pressed against his cock through his pants, drawing a harsh groan from him.

Not human. Not fully human, anyway. No human could ever have this kind of effect on him. She *became* his air and, without her, he drowned. Sebastian bit down on one cuff, ripped the button off to free his hand. Instead of stopping Willow's ministrations, he speared his fingers into her thick, gray mane and buried his nose in it at her temple. Her scent was like a teasing hint of winter on a hot summer day. It somehow forced his lungs to expand farther, breathe her in deeper.

Willow squeezed, and the breath he'd taken exploded out of him on a "*Ha!*" that forced every last molecule of air out of his body, and made him breathe her in again like an addict desperate for another hit, helplessly thinking, *What are you?*

The button on his pants came free. The zipper slid down. Willow pulled him out, her cool hands sliding up and down in a slow, teasing caress. Down to the base, pushing against his loins as if to get more of him. Up to the head—*fuck!*—*around* the head. He licked at her skin, molding her breasts in his hands, rocking his hips into her grasp at the same time.

Not enough. Yanking her hips to the very edge of the vanity, he shoved his hand between her legs, played his fingers over her slick flesh, tormenting her with the lightest of touches to pay her back in kind. Willow moaned and somehow, without her saying a word, he knew exactly what she needed. He knew exactly how to touch her to get her off and, gods, he was tempted.

But this wasn't some healer-prescribed treatment for his curse or an accidental, magic-induced fuck against the wall. This was all Sebastian. For the first time since before he'd even been old enough to know what the fuck he was doing, Sebastian was fully in control of his body. He knew exactly what he wanted, and how to get it, and what he wanted was hours, not minutes. He wanted this to last him a fucking lifetime and wipe out years of awkward, humiliating, agonizing memories.

So when Willow arched her back to raise her breasts higher, he hunched over her to bring his mouth level with her nipple, but instead of sucking on it the way she wanted him to, he breathed a warm puff of air against it and watched it pucker tighter. Watched delicate gooseflesh spread across her skin. Waited for the first hint of those swirling blue lines he knew would appear. Those symbols were his weathervane; he wanted to see her body covered with them.

Sebastian breathed on her other breast and Willow's hands tightened on him in reflex. He dug his heels into the floor, gritted his teeth and stubbornly refused to come. "Not going to control me that easily, *víla*. We do this *my* way."

She smiled in a way that was half tease, half challenge. "I haven't heard that word in ages."

"It suits you." He put his open mouth around her nipple, barely a touch, before withdrawing again. "You don't just work magic; you *are* magic. Just like the faery nymphs of old."

"A *víla* was also said to be beautiful beyond man's comprehension," she retorted with enough bitter vehemence to make him straighten face-to-face with her again.

"But you are."

Her pale skin heated with a flush. "Don't," she said.

"It's a compliment," he insisted, confused by the sudden heating of her hands on him. Even more so by the way his ardent desire cooled at the feel of it.

She pulled away, looked sideways. "It's a lie." With a butterfly touch of her hands, she brushed him aside and slid off the counter to the floor. "Believe me, I am well aware of what I look like, and 'beautiful' is not it." When she bowed her head and clutched a wild strand of her gray hair, Sebastian's joints locked with the precursor of pain.

"What can I do to convince you otherwise?" His voice was hoarse as he rubbed at his chest. It felt frozen and on fire at the same time.

Willow faced the bath and gave him her back, puffs of steam lovingly swirling around her as her shoulders drooped. "I'd like to finish my bath in privacy. Please."

Game over, champ. You fucking blew it. And the worst part was, he had no idea how.

Sebastian hunched his back to subtly stretch out his vertebrae to relieve the aching tension in his spine. He was sore all over, in ways that had nothing to do with his physical self. "I'm sorry," he said, at a loss for any other solution.

Willow stepped into the bath and turned off the water. The bathroom was steamed up like a sauna, even with the door wide open, and it somehow felt painfully incongruent with her.

"I'll need to go make a few calls, but I won't be far. If you need anything, call down to the front desk." He took his time doing his pants back up, in case she felt like responding.

She didn't.

Sebastian nodded. *Fair enough.* He let himself out, closed the door, and stalked back over to their luggage, digging for Willow's miracle cure potion. After shaking the bottle the way she usually did, he poured himself a dose and downed it from the hotel-issued glass, but the relief he so desperately needed didn't come. Sebastian waited for it, holding his breath, but there was no change, and the longer he stood there, the stiffer his joints became.

Something definitely wasn't right. Cursing through gritted teeth, he set the empty glass aside and snatched up his phone. Then he pulled on a T-shirt, stuffed the key card in his back pocket, and stalked out of the room on bare feet already dialing Declan.

Willow floated through Helegert's hallways like the ghost she'd been called all her life. She had no sense of herself; couldn't feel the floor beneath her feet; couldn't see her breath mist in the icy winter night. Faint strains of music called to her, and Willow followed the melody all the way to the grand ballroom.

Inside, beautiful couples draped in their finest twirled around the dance floor in an unbroken stream of color. The parade of smiling faces filled her with happiness at first, but the longer she watched them, the more she felt unease creep up behind her.

All those smiles were nothing but blank masks that turned more grotesque by the moment. Faces sheened with the gleam of porcelain; smiles froze too sharp, too red; eyes widened and rounded into glittering buttons.

The cold unease kissing the back of her neck turned into a rhythm: inhale, exhale. Frost crept out along the walls and floor, and the dancers lost their fluid grace. Their movements became choppy, broken, and unnatural, like the puppets they were and had always been. Their strings yanked them this way and that, making them trip and slam into one another. An arm broke off, hanging loosely from a man's shoulder. A foot slid across the floor, slowing to a stop before Willow.

She bent down to pick it up and saw her own reflection in the sheen of ice. Hair as white as snow, skin as pale as death… A ghost haunting a castle of broken toys and shattered dreams. "This is my legacy." The pride and love she'd always felt in her duty of maintaining Helegert didn't come. Instead, deep sadness suffused her for the broken toy she herself had become.

The cold entity at her back drew closer, its chill settling over her like a cold, comforting blanket. **You belong,** *it seemed to say.*

Willow looked out over the dance floor that had frozen over completely, the couples arrested in eternal waking sleep and desperately sought something else. Another choice. A way out. She sought the man who blazed hot enough to thaw her, but he was nowhere to be seen.

"Helloooooo!" she called out.

Elloooooo, *her own voice echoed back.*

"Helloooooo!" she tried again.

Elloooooo. Elloooooo. Elloooooo…

A cold draft snaked its arms around her, pulling her back into the illusion, giving her haunting strains of music to soothe away her doubts. When she tried to turn away, the music grew louder, forcing her back toward the puppets as they jerked and stumbled into a sinister waltz, and Willow panicked. "No!" She whirled around and ran with everything she had as, behind her, the castle squealed.

Willow didn't dare risk a glance. She couldn't bear to see the boulders tumbling down as the keep crumbled at her heels. She couldn't stomach the thought of her home dying, but she refused to yield to its hold on her. She would not give her life to keep standing. She would not die in its stead!

Ice cracked and groaned all around her, the floor sprouted fissures that went straight down into hell. Willow leaped over them, praying her footing didn't fail her, even as she stared ahead at the massive front doorway slowly swinging closed. Sunshine blazed just beyond it, bright green grass beckoned to her with its sharp, clean scent.

She focused on that promise, ran as fast as her tired legs would go, still searching for the one thing that could save her. She could almost see it, like a mirage wavering just out of reach. A core of swirling fire within a powerful chest. Arms open in welcome, a smile gracing the most beautiful face she had ever beheld. "Sebastian."

Merely speaking his name made him real, and so blessedly solid.

But the roar of destruction was gaining on her, frost nipping at her heels, shards of ice cutting her feet raw and bloody. She slipped and fell, mere inches from the door that kept closing. "Move," she commanded herself on a growl that cracked like a glacier in the spring. "Move!"

She moved. Debris rained down on her, battering her legs and back. She kept going, digging her fingers into the wooden threshold so hard she felt splinters stab under her nails. Willow ignored the pain, dragged herself across, cringing when the doors brushed the sides of her foot as they slammed shut.

She was out.

Battered, bleeding, and exhausted, Willow pushed herself upright, taking solace in Sebastian's smile before she made herself look at what she'd done. The door she'd crawled through vibrated with the echo of its slamming shut.

And behind it, Helegert was gone. Nothing but dust and rubble.

With a desperate moan, Willow whirled around to throw herself into her savior's arms—

—only to find he was nowhere to be seen.

Willow woke with a start, water sloshing over the edge of the tub. Shaken to her core, disoriented and unsteady, Willow righted her spectacles on her nose and looked around the unfamiliar bathroom as memory slowly returned. She was in a hotel, on her way to Kesteran.

She'd left Helegert.

Part of Willow felt like a traitor to her ancestors for daring to step foot off the property, but another part of her felt so very relieved. The exhausting emotional battle with herself made her bones turn to jelly.

With a groan, she pulled the plug to drain the tub and carefully stepped out. She dried herself and bundled up in a plush robe. Sebastian would be waiting out there to discuss her irrational break with sanity. How was she supposed to explain?

He'd called her beautiful. What a joke.

It shouldn't have hurt, of course, but somehow, his words had struck her like a frost grenade straight through her chest. They'd been empty words, goaded by whatever her wicked magic had wrought on him. And yes, dammit, it had hurt.

Because Willow knew that if it weren't for her healing having gone wrong, he never would have said such a thing to her. No one would.

The boy who'd taken her virginity certainly hadn't. He'd called her frigid, said he never should have taken his friends' bet, and left her there in the stables behind Icerton Inn to walk back to Helegert alone, with the blood of her maidenhead still drying on her thighs.

Neither had the one a year later, who'd asked to paint her portrait. To him, she'd been curious and unique. But after endless hours of posing for him, and a few innocent kisses, he'd left, and she'd never seen him again.

Beautiful…

Willow backtracked and faced the mirror, forcing herself to confront what was real. The mirror didn't disappoint her with an empty lie. It showed her the truth. She was skinny to the point of being scrawny for her frame, all awkwardly long arms and legs wrapped in pallid skin. She had no grace at all, social or otherwise; no feminine wiles, guiles, or enticements. Her hips were straight, her breasts were small—she was a walking coat hanger with a thick mane of gray hair that refused to be tamed.

Nothing but an upside-down mop. A dusty one.

Frustrated, she snatched up a hotel-issued comb and started dragging it through her hair. Within moments, so many of its plastic teeth had broken off, it became useless. Undaunted, Willow grabbed handfuls of her hair and braided it tightly down the center of her head from front to back, and into a sturdy queue that dangled between her shoulder blades.

"There."

Still a walking coat hanger, but at least her hair was presentable.

In no way satisfied, Willow reached up, hesitated, then scowled at herself and resolutely took off her spectacles, folding them on the vanity. The world, including her reflection, turned into one huge blur. Somehow, that made her feel marginally better. Without the harsh, unforgiving focus of sharp vision, her blurred shape looked almost pleasing. She turned to the side, then the other side and her reflection's copied movements looked more fluid than she knew herself to be.

One hand on the bathrobe belt, she contemplated taking it off, then shook her head at herself. Safer not to. All those angles where curves should be... It wasn't for nothing that people always said the dress made the woman.

How happy King Marcus will be to meet his scarecrow cousin.

Beautiful...

What a cruel, cruel joke.

Willow turned away from the mirror and braced herself before opening the door and emerging out into the hotel room, still having no idea what to say to Sebastian.

She was spared the effort.

Sebastian wasn't there.

CHAPTER 14

The wake-up call the next morning couldn't have come early enough. Sebastian, already awake, snatched up the phone and dropped it back into its cradle to stop the ringing. He hadn't slept more than a couple of hours, with his body wound tight and his mind replaying last night over and over to figure out what the hell had gone wrong.

Willow had been asleep when he'd come back after checking in with everyone back home and making sure everything would be ready for their arrival. She'd braided her hair again, and the sight of it had made something in his chest clench and pop painfully. Sebastian had had half a mind to wake her up and make her take it down, make her tell him what he'd done wrong.

He'd stopped himself only because he knew she'd need all the rest she could get before they reached Kesteran. Marcus and Snow had been busy in his absence, dealing with some peripheral shit that made Sebastian's little outing take a back seat to important crown business, but now that they knew for a fact he was coming back with Willow, the preparations would begin.

Snow wanted to welcome Willow properly, with all the pomp and circumstance that befitted a royal Sturmgard descendant. There would be balls and feasts to celebrate, and elaborate performances, processions, and fireworks, all of which Snow expected Willow to attend with a smile on her face.

She hadn't let him get a word in edgewise to tell her that was the last thing Willow needed or wanted. His warning text message to Marcus afterward had been brushed off as nonsense. Of course, Willow would love it all.

Right.

Willow stirred on her bed, stretching out of the covers before she sat up, knuckling her eyes. The morning sun made her pale skin look almost pearlescent. More beautiful than any woman he'd ever seen—including Zorana and Snow.

And she'd reacted as if he'd struck her when he'd told her so last night.

"Good morrow," he said.

She squinted at him, started to smile, then caught herself and replied with caution, "Good morrow."

"Hungry?"

Willow shrugged. "A little." She caught her braid to fiddle with, looking around at anything but him.

Bones creaking, Sebastian sat up and took stock of his body. Still sore. Still humming like a beehive. Still nowhere near the agony he'd struggled with for half his life. And still nowhere near as painful as the silence stretching on. Out of sheer desperation, he said, "Your glasses are right there on the nightstand, in case you're wondering."

"Oh." Willow retrieved them and blinked her owl eyes at him. "I thought I left them in the bathroom."

He shrugged, rolling his shoulder in the same motion. "You did. I thought there would be less chance of them getting broken out here." Since he hadn't seen a spare pair anywhere when she'd packed for the trip, it made that set the most valuable thing she owned.

She offered a half smile in answer. "So what's the plan for the day?"

"I ordered the luggage to be shipped ahead and reserved a car. Should get us into Kesteran by tonight if we step on it." He'd passed on the roomier models in favor of a fast little sports car, sacrificing comfort for speed. The carriage ride that had taken him a full week to complete going north in shitty weather could be cut down to a quarter of that length with paved roads and a car that could get up to a hundred and fifty miles per hour.

Which was a very good thing, because Sebastian wasn't sure how much longer he could spend with Willow in a confined vehicle without losing his fucking mind. Sebastian still craved Willow with an intensity that shook him to his core, and he was fast approaching a point where he feared he wouldn't be able to hold back any longer.

She looked like a vision from his dreams, sitting there on the plush bed, and he couldn't stop imagining what it'd be like to join her across the small divide, strip that godsawful chemise from her, and lay her down on the plush bed. Despite her morning blush, he knew her skin would be just as cool as before, and that she would taste like winter's first snow, and the only thing keeping him rooted in place was knowing that, right at this moment, she didn't want him anywhere near her.

The sooner they made it to the castle where other people had a vested interest in keeping her company, the better. He hoped.

"When do we leave?"

"Whenever you're ready," he replied. "Stretch your legs while you can. Once we get on the road, I don't plan on stopping except for bathroom breaks."

Willow nodded, absorbing what he told her, then moved the covers aside and swung her feet down to the floor.

"Listen, about yesterday—"

"Forgotten," she cut in, making him gnash his teeth.

"Not by me." He sat up, mirroring her and tried like hell to meet her gaze. "You were right there with me, every step. And then you weren't. What did I do that upset you so?"

Willow shook her head, her gaze stubbornly stuck on the foot of his bed. "Nothing."

"Liar."

She huffed. "I mean it. You didn't do anything. I'm the one who… Anyway, let's just forget it, okay? Never happened."

She looked like she'd rather be anywhere but there, still playing with the end of that damned braid. Without thinking, he reached out to take her hand. "Willow—"

She jumped off the bed and danced out of reach before he could touch her. "You know, I just realized, I am starving. Does the hotel have a restaurant?"

Caught off guard by the quicksilver change, Sebastian belatedly lowered his hand. "Of course—"

"Great! Can we do breakfast soon, then? You probably want to get back to Kesteran yesterday. Things to do, I imagine, people to see. I won't be a minute." She moved as she talked, digging through the trunk and emerging with her arms full of clothes. "I'll wash up and get dressed and then we can be on our way." The door slammed shut between them.

"All right, then."

That went fucking well.

Willow dropped her clothes on the floor and slapped her hands over her face. Gods, could this possibly get any worse? What in the world was wrong with her?

Shake it off. Get ahold of yourself. She'd promised to be done quickly, and that meant she couldn't stand around and wait for the earth to swallow her up so she wouldn't have to go out there again. *Deep breath. It's nothing.*

Willow shook herself off like a wet dog. She made use of the toilet, then washed up and undid her braid to attempt yet again to brush it into some sort of order. As sore as her scalp was from sleeping with her hair in a braid, returning it to that state again was not an option. Instead, she tied it loosely at her nape. Good enough for the time being.

Sebastian knocked and she jumped. "Almost finished!"

On the other side of the door Sebastian cleared his throat. "I, uh, got you some things to wear from the lobby gift shop."

Willow paused. "What?"

"Nothing against your wardrobe," he said quickly, "but I saw what you packed. It's all thick wool gowns and all of them too big for you."

Walking coat hanger. Right.

"You'll end up overheating and won't be able to move freely. I thought you might want something lighter, is all."

Willow looked at the faded crimson overdress that on its own weighed at least ten pounds. He was right. She hated the very idea of putting the damned thing on.

"Anyway, I'll just leave it out here. You can wear it, or return it. Whatever. Your choice."

"Thank you," she said, unsure what to do with this unexpected stroke of thoughtfulness.

"Welcome," he replied. "I'll go down to the restaurant to grab us a table for breakfast. Meet you down there."

Willow nodded as his boot thumps sounded his exit from the room. She waited for a few seconds more before she opened the door and retrieved the small stack of clothes he'd bought for her. Soft, stretchy leggings, a strappy, fitted white undershirt, and a thin, billowy blouse that buttoned in the front like a dress shirt, but flared down from the shoulders. It was so long it'd reach down to her knees and so thin the undershirt was a necessity to preserve modesty.

The leggings and undershirt hugged her like glove, the stretchy materials molding to her form almost too well. Even with the billowy overshirt covering her from shoulder to knee, Willow felt scandalously naked, but she knew she'd be grateful later on. The morning was already much hotter than what she was used to, and it would only get worse along the way.

The knowledge didn't give her an ounce of confidence as she slinked out of the room and down the stairs to the lobby. Keeping to the walls and shadows, she found the restaurant by navigating helpful directional signs and located Sebastian at a table by the window.

He stood as soon as he saw her, and pulled out her chair for her, slowly looking her up and down. His bold inspection made heat creep up to Willow's cheeks. "How do I look?"

Sebastian appeared to give the matter some thought. "Something's not quite right," he mused, then reached around and undid the tie holding her hair in place. "There. Now you're flawless."

Anger resurged, battling with secret pleasure, and not a small amount of embarrassment, and she froze, unsure of which to act on first.

Sebastian shrugged. "You asked. I answered truthfully." He inclined his head, indicating for her to take a seat.

She did, but her nerves wouldn't stop buzzing. She felt exposed, and even though they were two of only ten or so patrons in the restaurant, she kept expecting the others to stare and whisper. Ducking her head, she tugged on a strand of her hair, pulling it over her shoulder to hide her face.

"Do you know what you want to eat?"

"I should have dyed it," she muttered. "I didn't think. I had all the ingredients at Helegert. I should have dyed it."

Sebastian's menu tapped down on the table, then his fingers brushed under her chin, coaxing her to look up. "I like your hair," he said, staring hard into her eyes as if to somehow force her to believe him. "It's unique, and it suits you."

"It's gray," she reminded him flatly.

"It's silver," he countered. "And soft, and shiny, and smells like Midwinter and magic." He released her chin to take her hand. "Stop fidgeting. It makes me twitchy." Acting like that concluded the conversation, he reopened his menu with his free hand, but never released his hold on her with the other and, as he read through their options for breakfast, his thumb absently brushed back and forth across her wrist.

She stared at him, waiting for him to realize what he was doing, but he looked so casual and comfortable, as if it was all perfectly normal. Even that awful tether between them had settled, no longer tugging at her quite as hard. Willow didn't know what to make of it. "Midwinter and magic?"

His mouth twitched in a smile. "No upset, no arguments. I think we're making progress."

What did that mean?

The arrival of their waiter put an end to their conversation for the time being. Willow let it go, not knowing she wouldn't get another chance to address it.

CHAPTER 15

Willow didn't realize how long they drove until the sun dipped low enough to glare at her through the side window. Her hopes of a safe night's rest at a roadside hotel in deference to the dark got dashed before she could even voice them. The car had lights bright enough to illuminate the road more than a dozen feet ahead, which Sebastian appeared to consider sufficient for them to keep going.

It took several more hours after it got completely dark for them to reach the outskirts of Kesteran. Within the city, Sebastian finally slowed down, which allowed her time to admire the architecture and landscaping of a city that, by Sebastian's own accounts, had been all but destroyed only two short years ago.

The mobile phone in a cup holder between them buzzed again. Sebastian glanced at it but didn't pick it up. He'd been doing that all day; hadn't even checked it when they'd stopped for lunch. There had to be at least fifty messages waiting for him by now. Although she was grateful he didn't allow himself to get distracted while driving, Willow still heard herself asking, "Don't you need to answer that?"

"We're almost there. Whoever it is can wait ten more minutes."

She shrugged, too exhausted to argue. "If you say so."

Past a beautifully manicured park lit with a myriad of faery globes, they turned onto a drive and stopped in front of a gigantic wrought iron gate. A guard came out of his booth, and Sebastian handed him something. "Wait there," the guard said and disappeared back inside. After a short conversation on the phone, he returned whatever Sebastian had given him and instructed, "If you drive around back to the private garage, an attendant will escort you to their Majesties' receiving rooms."

Sebastian swore, but nodded and accelerated through the gate.

"What's wrong?"

"Looks like you get to meet your cousin a little sooner than I expected. I was hoping they'd at least let you settle down, get some sleep before an official audience."

Alarm spiked through her, making her sit up straighter. "I'm not ready! I'm not dressed, and I'm tired, and—"

"I know," he said, then caught her hand as she furtively tried to finger-comb her hair. "Relax. It's almost midnight. As eccentric as they are, even Snow and Marcus aren't crazy enough to make a big deal right as you walk in the door. I think Marcus is just eager to meet you, that's all."

He stopped next to an open door where a tired-looking, hastily put together young man waited for them beneath a faery globe as a deep bell tolled midnight somewhere far above them. "Any wise words of advice?"

Sebastian squeezed her hand and pressed a quick kiss to her knuckles. "Remember he's more afraid of you than you are of him."

She frowned. "What? Why?"

The attendant came out to open Willow's door, then led them inside with assurances that their belongings would be taken care of.

Willow clutched Sebastian's arm as they walked down the hallway, her mind absorbed with thoughts of Helegert. Her home had always been meant to look this grand and elegant. Willow just hadn't been able to find anyone willing to help her restore it, and couldn't manage it on her own.

Maybe King Marcus would help. Surely, a royal order could get a proper crew out to the keep. Helegert would be back to its former glory in no time. Perhaps having relatives really would be a good thing.

At the end of their path, the boy opened a double door and bowed back for them to enter ahead of him. She could already see a man's shadow moving back and forth as its owner paced around the corner and her feet stuck at the threshold.

Sebastian looked down at her. "Remember, you're an honored guest. Marcus is a good man. You have nothing to be afraid of."

"Will you stay with me?"

"Begging your pardon," the boy said, still bowed over and looking at the carpet. "Her Majesty has asked me to convey Master Sebastian to her office."

Sebastian huffed in irritation. "Now?"

"I believe it was her Majesty's wish to allow his Majesty a few private moments with Lady Faithblade."

Willow whimpered, but a royal order was a royal order. She made her fingers unclench to let go of Sebastian, and a panic threatened to overtake her as the last contact between them broke. "I'll be fine," she whispered, more to herself than anything else.

Sebastian's hand ghosted across her cheek. "I have no doubt of that."

Then he was gone, walking away after the boy with long, determined strides, leaving Willow to face the king of Valefort all alone.

Clenching her hands in her long shirt, Willow took a deep breath and stepped into the room.

Instead of an aging figure of authority with a long white beard and an ermine cloak she'd expected, King Marcus of Valefort was the epitome of handsome youth. His blond hair was tousled, his brown eyes wide and staring at her from a face that must have inspired many a girl's dreams of happily ever after. Dressed casually in jeans and a shirt with the sleeves rolled up past his elbows, he looked as if he'd thrown everything on in a hurry to meet her, and his feet, she was amused to note, were stuffed into floppy slippers that trailed stray threads left and right.

"Cousin Willow," he said, his deep voice rich with surprise. Then, to her utter shock, he bowed low from the waist. "Please accept my humble welcome and my deepest sympathies."

Willow remembered her manners and curtsied. "Thank you for receiving me upon my arrival. I am most grateful for your hospitality."

King Marcus smiled with genuine warmth, but his eyes were sad, somehow. "You must be exhausted after your trip. Shall we sit? Would you care for some refreshments?" He indicated a pillowy armchair opposite his own and a platter of cold cuts and breads.

Willow nodded her acceptance and took a seat.

"First, I would like to apologize on behalf of myself, and my family for the rift that's kept us apart this long. Please know that if I had even the slightest inkling that you were alive, and in Valefort no less, I would have sought you sooner. I'm just grateful Sebastian brought you out before tragedy struck."

Icy dread seized her by the base of her spine. "What tragedy?"

King Marcus frowned. "Hasn't Sebastian told you?"

Numb from the top of her head to the tips of her toes, Willow slowly shook her head in the negative.

"We've been trying to reach you for hours. He must not have gotten our messages."

No, he'd been too busy ignoring his buzzing phone. "What's happened?" she asked, barely above a whisper, her mind screaming that she already knew the answer, and it was all her fault.

King Marcus shifted in his seat, leaned forward and rested his elbows on his knees. He looked like he might want to take her hand, but when she curled her fingers tighter into her stomach, he appeared to reconsider. "We tried to reach you as soon as we heard, to make sure you were all right. This morning, a messenger from Icerton called in to report a rumbling boom of noise that shook the ground for miles. When the noise stopped, they went out to investigate and… Willow, I'm so sorry to tell you, but it appears that Helegert Keep has…disintegrated. They found nothing left, just a mountain of boulders and rubble."

The ringing started in her left ear but soon spread to her right like a two-tone siren that wouldn't let up. Willow was aware of her cousin telling her all the proper things, about how he regretted the tragedy, and how grateful he was that she'd made it to Kesteran safe and sound, and how her home was here now, with her family…

Willow absorbed none of it. She heard a wheezing, whimpering sound and realized it was coming from her. Her freezing hands stuck in cauldrons of heat, and she blinked down to see them caught in the king's larger, swarthier ones. She registered the concern on his face, but couldn't hear what he was saying any longer past the roar of falling boulders. The cozy room blew away on a frigid wind, and suddenly she was back in her dream of Helegert, running for that open door, her beacon of safety, as the keep fell apart all around her.

And she knew.

She knew that everything her mother, and her mother, and her mother before her had said about the keep had been true. They'd poured their lives into Helegert, imbued it with their magic, and it had stood only as long as one of them had remained. It had been Willow's duty to care for Helegert, and she'd shirked it, selfishly turning away to run after an impossible idea.

Only, in her dream, that idea had vanished as surely as Helegert itself.

"Sebastian," she murmured through numb lips. "I need to see Sebastian right away."

The second Sebastian walked through the door, he got slammed with an armful of tousled queendom. "You're here!" Snow said with so much relief, it made his arms go leaden with dread. He hugged her back with uncharacteristic awkwardness, sending a questioning look at Declan, who gave a grim nod of greeting in response.

"Uh, yeah. As promised. Mission accomplished."

She stepped back, making a visible effort to compose herself. "I spoke to Declan, and he said you had concerns regarding Willow's cure."

"So you summoned us both to double check the results?" Not that he minded. Saved him a trip, as a matter of fact. But the healer looked so put-out to have been summoned in the middle of the night, his bedside manner was sure to be utter shit. And he wasn't the gentlest of healers to begin with.

"In short, yes," she returned, unfazed. "There have been too many false negatives for you in the past. I want to make sure this cure sticks before we start celebrating. And, given recent events, I want to make extra sure you're up for active duty."

"Okay, what the hell is going on?"

Declan turned one big hand palm-up toward a foldable gurney someone had dragged in.

"Fine, don't tell me. Just so happens I'm glad I don't have to wake you up myself." He sat on the gurney, rolling his shoulders. For a couple of hours there, driving across the countryside, he'd felt almost fully healed. He'd been able to breathe again the way he had right after Willow's spell. Now the old stiffness was back, along with the fear that it was all too good to be true.

Declan laid one hand on top of Sebastian's head and one on his left shoulder, his healer's magic washing over Sebastian. "Tell me everything."

He reviewed everything for Declan and Snow's benefit, from Willow's initial diagnosis, to the three attempts at removing the curse, to the strange side effects that seemed to come and go in random intervals. He held back nothing, up to and including his inexplicable attraction to Willow, but he studiously avoided Declan's and Snow's gazes while he spoke.

Declan hummed thoughtfully, then adjusted the position of his hands on Sebastian and sent his odd magic probing deeper. As essentially a byproduct of a spell gone wrong, a Ravenskin was always born with powerful magic of his or her own, but it was different, warped, and operated on principles that were turned on their head when compared to natural magic workers like Willow. As a result, Declan perceived magic differently and often found a different, more effective solution to a problem.

"Give it to me straight, how badly did I get myself fucked up this time?"

Declan frowned. "I'm…not sure."

A long string of foul curses spilled out of Sebastian. "Something got left behind, didn't it?" He should have known a curse that had stuck to him for a decade and a half wouldn't go down without a fight.

But instead of confirming his suspicion, Declan tilted his head and said, "I don't think so. But I can't tell what it is I'm looking at."

That didn't sound good. "Describe it."

"Wait." Declan pressed one hand flat over Sebastian's heart and pushed, physically and magically.

Sebastian jerked under the pressure that cut off his air and made his heart labor to keep beating. Whatever Declan was doing, it fucking *hurt*. He gripped the edges of the gurney and gasped out, "Stop. *Stop!*"

Declan released him immediately, and Sebastian slumped in his seat, gasping for air.

"What did you do?" Snow demanded, tilting up Sebastian's face to look into his eyes.

He brushed her aside. "I'm okay. I'm fine." Accepting the glass of water Declan offered, he downed the contents in one swallow and took a couple of minutes to catch his breath. Finally, he felt steady enough to think. "What the fuck!"

Declan stared at him as if Sebastian had insulted his ancestors. "That did not go the way it was supposed to."

"Yeah, no shit." This from their elegant monarch. "What were you trying to do, rip out his heart?"

Declan raised an eyebrow. "That's just it. That's what it felt like to me, too, but it shouldn't have."

Shit, that sounded serious. "I'm not gonna like this, am I?"

Declan sighed, crossing his massive arms over his chest. His silver eyes gleamed as he met Sebastian's gaze head-on. "The good news is that Zorana's curse appears to have been excised in its entirety."

"That's excellent!" Snow said. "You're healed."

"Throttle down, sweetheart," Sebastian advised as a cold weight of dread settled in the pit of his stomach. "Good news first means there's bad news, too." *But, gods, I don't want to hear it.* He was supposed to be thinking about what to do with all those years he never thought he'd have, and planning binge drinking outings, and reckless adventures, and all the other stupid shit he'd dreamed about. Sebastian had a decade and a half to make up for—he wanted his life back, godsdammit! He'd fucking earned that much, hadn't he?

"Unfortunately, yes," Declan said, and the bottom of Sebastian's stomach dropped out. "There's something else in its place now."

The room moved side to side as Sebastian numbly shook his head in denial. Even as his rational mind argued that he'd had his suspicions all along and the news was nothing more than a confirmation of what he'd already known, the part of him that had seized on his cure as the end of a lifetime of torment simply refused to accept it. Declan could be wrong. The symptoms could be a fluke, residual echoes, like Willow had said.

But the healer wouldn't be standing there now, watching Sebastian with that stoic reserve he always gave his terminal patients if it was something that simple.

Which could only mean one thing.

"A new curse?" His throat felt so tight he could barely speak the words, but as soon as he said them, Sebastian knew they were true. He felt it in his bones. Literally.

"We don't know that. It could—"

"Like hell we don't!" Sebastian exploded out of his seat, sending Snow stumbling away from him. "We know exactly what this is because there's only one thing it could be: Willow's magic. She didn't heal me. She just traded Zorana's leash for one she could control."

A hermit shunned by everyone within miles, she would have been desperate for companionship. And there Sebastian had been, feeling sorry for her. Gods, it made him sick to his stomach to even think about it. She'd used him. All that goofy charm and those quirky little habits of hers he'd thought were so fucking adorable had been nothing but a ruse to keep him from suspecting foul play.

And he'd been so desperate with hope he'd fallen for it, hook, line, and sinker. "Explains everything right there," he said, gritting his teeth against a wave of nausea. "Every last symptom, from the aches and stiffness to the attraction I just happened to have developed when I haven't felt anything like it in *fourteen years!*" Snow gasped, but Sebastian was too shaken up to care anymore. "There. I fucking solved it for you."

"Sebastian," Snow whispered, but didn't follow it up with anything else. There was nothing left to say.

"Can you remove it?" he asked Declan point blank.

"No," the healer replied without even pausing to think. "And I would not, even if I could."

The offhand betrayal sent Sebastian reeling back. His legs bumped against the gurney as he stared at one of the men he'd, up until now, considered family.

Reading his expression, Declan held up his hands in a peacekeeping gesture. "You must let me explain—"

"Go to hell," Sebastian rasped, shoving past Declan. He yanked open the door and stopped dead at the sight of Willow and Marcus coming toward him. They stopped at the same time and the moment froze suspended in a miasma of unspoken words.

Willow's expression changed in quicksilver progression from surprise, to understanding, to shame, and finally hurt. "Sebastian…"

"Save it for someone who gives a shit."

"Collins!" Marcus snapped, but Sebastian didn't care. He was already past them both and had no intention of ever looking back.

He hadn't when Zorana had stabbed her magical claws into him, he sure as shit wouldn't now.

Not even if it killed him.

Sebastian had a sick feeling in the pit of his stomach that this time, it just might.

CHAPTER 16

Asearing spear of lightning flashed down the tether, striking Willow with such force it sent her sobbing to her knees, and for a long time, she saw nothing but bright flashes of light amid total darkness; heard nothing but the broken sounds of grief and agony. She felt herself speaking a litany of heartfelt words, but couldn't make sense of their shape on her tongue. All she knew was that she'd lost *everything*.

Even the thing she'd had no right to have in the first place.

Eventually, the sensation of a large hand pressing across the top of her chest registered and the miasma cleared. She found herself lying prone, staring up at a man with skin as black as pitch that somehow... shone with darkness patterned like feathers, an impossibility compounded by his glowing silver eyes that should have reflected like mirrors, but instead absorbed light.

"Slowly now," he said in a deep, deep voice, his mouth barely moving with the sounds. She felt his magic inside her, a sensation at once invasive and comforting, but altogether unfamiliar.

Then more faces appeared and she struggled to match them with names. King Marcus of Valefort—she'd met him earlier and remembered his solicitous bafflement and genuine concern. It was still there now, as if he truly cared for her well-being, though they'd only just met.

That meant the other person had to be his wife. Queen Snow White was almost too beautiful to comprehend. She looked like a living porcelain doll with large, soulful eyes, and a thick mane of hair as black as the healer's skin, only lacking the magical underlay. "How do you feel?" she asked, and Willow shattered all over again.

"I am so sorry." Her voice was hoarse, breaking as the shivers started anew. "I didn't mean to. I tried so hard to fix everything and—"

"Take a breath for me," said the man with glowing skin and unglowing eyes. "Nice and slow." His magic wove in with the words, making her limbs feel heavy and her frantic heartbeat to slow. "Very good. Keep breathing just like that. There's no need to upset yourself. No one is blaming you for anything. Sebastian told us what he knew, but I would like to hear your version of it, if you please. I think it's safe to assume that we all want the same thing, and the more we know, the better."

Willow nodded. Yes, he was right, of course. She could feel the Power in his words and in his touch, and it told her he was a master at his own craft. The words came out with difficulty as shame colored her cheeks with a heated brush, but she forced herself to speak them. They might not have blamed her at first, but they would eventually, and who knew what kind of punishment the royal couple decided to mete out then?

When she finished, the man whose name she still didn't know helped her sit up and held her steady until her head stopped spinning. It was only then that she noticed bright sunlight streaming in through the window. Dawn. No wonder she was so exhausted.

"What do you mean by 'tether'?" the healer asked.

Willow looked down at shimmering, flickering line of magic stretching out of her chest to a distance of several feet where it tapered off so thin it became invisible. "It's right here. Can't you see it?"

The healer shook his head. "No. I didn't see anything in Sebastian, either. Only the mass of magic inside him."

Willow gaped at him. "How can that be?" She focused back on the tether and plucked it with her will. It strummed hard with a yearning so powerful and painful it almost made her pass out again.

"Whoa!" King Marcus caught her as she listed to the side and braced her against him until she could keep her own seat. "What just happened?"

"Declan?" Queen Snow asked with a worried frown.

"I didn't See anything, but I sure as hell *felt* something."

"And?" King Marcus pushed.

The healer took a slow, deep breath, then let it out on a big sigh. "Truthfully, I don't know."

"Which means," King Marcus retorted, "you have twenty ideas you want to test out before you commit to an answer."

Declan dared to glare at the regent and growl, "I don't like your tone."

"And I don't like your stalling," the king replied with equal venom. "Spit it out already." That he would tolerate such insubordination at all baffled Willow.

Queen Snow put a hand on each man's arm. "Guys, please. It's Sebastian."

Both men visibly unclenched, and finally, Declan nodded. "Whatever happened during the extraction of Zorana's curse feels just as complicated as the curse itself. There is no Darkness in it. It feels more like an unfinished soul spell fueled by raw magic."

Willow buried her face in her hands, dislodging her glasses. Soul spells were never one-sided. Which meant the solution would be complicated, and odds were good none of them would like it, least of all Sebastian.

Then she remembered the powerful urge she'd been feeling and fighting for days. "Could a kiss complete the spell?"

"It's possible," Declan allowed. "But without knowing what the spell actually is, we can't know what its completion will mean."

"And right now, Sebastian would rather strangle me than kiss me, anyway." She couldn't even imagine approaching him with such a suggestion. "Which means we're at an impasse."

The royal couple and their healer exchanged a grave look among them in a wordless debate Willow wasn't privy to. There appeared to be a decision, and then King Marcus winced and said, "We could draw straws," which earned him glares from the two others.

Willow had no idea what to make of these strange people. They followed none of the official court protocols her mother and grandmother had drilled into her for years. "There is one thing," she said timidly to reclaim their attention. "I know I have no right to ask for anything, under the circumstances, but…"

It was Snow who reached out and took her hand, squeezing lightly. "Willow, you're family. Whatever it is, it's already yours."

She smiled back, grateful for the sentiment, but not really believing a word of it. She framed her request as humbly and unselfishly as possible. "Back in Helegert, Sebastian and I found some old documents and journals written by my foremothers. I thought maybe there might be a clue in them about who sired Alvina's daughter. If he had any magic at all, it might have altered mine. Maybe it could give us another clue to a solution?"

"It's possible," Declan said. "You inherited your family's unique abilities, which aren't very well understood to begin with. If another strain had been added to the mix, it could very well have altered your physical and magical makeup. It's worth investigating. Have you brought these documents with you?"

"Yes. Sebastian insisted on it."

King Marcus nodded. "I'll get our people on it right away."

"In the meantime," Queen Snow said, "why don't I show you to your rooms? You've been through so much the last couple of days, you must be exhausted."

Willow nodded and meekly followed the Queen of Valefort, already knowing she wouldn't sleep a wink.

CHAPTER 17

Sebastian waded through a waist-high snow drift, chasing the wailing wind across an endless expanse of white. But it wasn't the wind making that sound, it was something else. Something that burned like acid across his conscience, driving him on when he could barely move at all. He was getting closer. The snow drift shallowed out, the going became easier, and at last Sebastian stood before a massive wooden door.

Only the castle it should have been attached to was gone. The stone wall perimeter that should have enclosed a slice of summer nearby was nowhere to be seen. There was nothing left of any of it, except that doorway holding up a thick, wooden frame, and a single layer of ragged mooring boulders around it.

And the wailing.

Sebastian lifted the heavy door knocker and let it fall. The crack of noise it produced echoed with the rumble of an unseen avalanche, but no one answered it. He put his shoulder to the portal and shoved with everything he had, managing to budge it a few inches open. Barely enough to squeeze through.

On the other side, the same barren scene stretched as far as he could see, broken up with piles of dark stones here and there. And about fifty yards away, a woman knelt in the snow, blending in so well he would *have missed her, were it not for her howls of grief.*

Sebastian's heart constricted in a painful spasm that yanked on him so hard he stumbled forward. It demanded he go to her, and he was helpless to stop himself. Her hair had turned pure white, and her skin glistened like the snow around him. Elegant and regal in a beautiful blue and silver satin gown, she looked nothing like herself, and yet this was the true Willow; the way she would have looked if time and circumstances had been kinder.

What are you?

Did it even matter anymore?

Her heartbreak pulsed in a thick aura around Sebastian, suffocating him, and he knew it was merely a fraction of what she felt. Hurting with her, Sebastian sank to his haunches and reached out, but his ghostly hand passed right through her shoulder.

He couldn't stand to see her like this. "Willow, look at me."

She quieted and looked up, and Sebastian lost his breath. Her face was tattooed with blue markings that traced the line of her brow and curled around her temples. Frozen droplets of her tears glittered like diamonds on her cheeks, and her eyes blazed with amber light as she stared unseeing straight through him. "Look at you?" she repeated, "But you're not here. You never were."

"I'm right here!"

"I'm alone," she said in a hollow voice that gave him chills. "I'll always be alone..."

Sebastian leaned forward, to put his arms around her, but in this world, he didn't exist. Like cold mist on a snowy field, he melted around Willow without ever making contact, and dropped right into a dark chasm on her other side.

The sensation of falling woke Sebastian a split second before he hit the floor next to his bed. With a pained groan he rolled onto his back and stayed there while his heart rate returned to a normal rhythm.

That was the third time he'd had that eerie fucking dream, and just like the other times, it left him chilled to the bone. He grabbed for the alarm clock on his nightstand. Six in the morning. The sun was coming up, which meant it was time for Sebastian to get his shit together.

He sleepwalked through his morning shower and a nondescript

breakfast, then thought about turning on his computer and checking his email but decided not to. His phone lay on the floor where he'd tossed it five days ago after turning it off to stop the incessant buzz of incoming calls and messages. Sebastian didn't want to talk to anyone. He didn't even want to acknowledge the world at large still existed out there.

He no longer cared.

Liar, his conscience accused.

Sebastian ignored it. Just like he'd ignored the notes shoved through his mail slot, and the royal messenger knocking at his door to invite him to the castle.

But Beau's visit yesterday was a little harder to ignore. Beau didn't often trouble himself to come out of his own head, let alone to make a house call. And the queen's master strategist hadn't even tried to talk sense into Sebastian, which somehow made his visit that much worse. He'd merely knocked, and when Sebastian had yelled at him to fuck off, he'd said the one thing that still bothered Sebastian today: "Do yourself a favor, and turn on the news."

Nothing else.

He'd known it would fester in Sebastian's mind until his own curiosity got the better of him.

He'd been right.

With a foul curse, Sebastian snatched up the TV remote and turned on the Valefort Crown Channel, his go-to for any news worth watching. Today, the pretty news anchor's face was grave as she read from a teleprompter while behind her a live video feed hissed with static.

"Once again," she was saying, *"We are showing you live footage of what remains after an undisclosed event caused the Helegert Castle of White Plains to collapse."*

Sebastian sat down hard on the edge of the coffee table.

"The keep was built in the era of King Alfred IV as a gift to his most favored mistress and was hailed a wonder of modern engineering for its time. Two centuries later, after sustaining major damage during the Battle of White Plains, it was abandoned and deemed no longer habitable. Our station has received reports that, despite this, the cas-

tle had, in fact, been inhabited in recent history, even up to the final collapse. These reports have not been substantiated. The ruins are now being searched, but so far, the crews have found nothing to suggest that someone might have been living on the premises—"

Sebastian hit the power button.

He stared at the dark TV monitor for what felt like hours, and when the walls started closing in on him, he got in his car, revved the engine, and gunned it down an endless country road.

Helegert was gone.

Sebastian tried to picture the keep as he'd first seen it, but his mind only conjured the snowy heap of stones from his dream, and Willow weeping in its center.

Willow.

Fuck, she had to be devastated.

Right on the heels of that hint of compassion came cold disdain. Willow was Marcus' cousin, and even without everything they'd left behind in Helegert, she still had a title and crates full of Zorana-era gold coins, which amounted to more money than ten people could spend in a hundred years. She'd be living large and breaking hearts in no time.

Sebastian slammed both hands against the steering wheel hard enough to honk the horn. He didn't fucking care! Not about what she did, or where she lived, and especially not about how she felt to have lost the only home she'd ever known.

The woman had lied to him, manipulated him, *cursed* him, and used him. Helegert falling down was nothing more than her due—and she was damned lucky he'd brought her out of there before it buried her. Sebastian almost laughed. *No good deed ever goes unpunished.*

An official summons waited for him when he returned late that afternoon, attached to the front door with the royal seal standing out at eye-level where he couldn't possibly miss it. Sebastian had half a mind to ignore it but, like it or not, he was still Queen Snow's vassal.

He snatched the folded piece of parchment and stormed inside, slamming the door behind him.

"It's for the trial." In the living room darkened by drawn shades,

Declan's form was almost invisible as he unfolded from his seat, his movements fluid and graceful like a panther on the prowl. "I got the same one. Snow is putting a Supreme Court Judge on trial, and we're all required to attend as a show of support."

Sebastian stamped out the flicker of interest at that bit of news. "Get out."

The back-stabbing son of a bitch didn't even flinch. "You know, the unfortunate thing about persistent curses? They carve out room for themselves, and when they're removed, they create a vacuum that sucks in whatever is nearby, whether it wants to go or not. It is, in a word, inescapable."

What the fuck was he talking about? "You're wasting your breath."

"And you're pissing me off."

The parchment crackled as it crumpled in Sebastian's fist, and the only thing stopping Sebastian from driving that fist into Declan's traitorous face was the twenty-foot distance between them. By the time Sebastian made it across, Declan would have leveled him.

The healer's eyes shone even brighter as his rarely-seen temper surged to the surface. "In all the years we have known each other, I have never seen you this stupid."

"If you're spoiling for a fight—"

"You would be more than happy to give it to me, right? I notice your back is straight. You're not limping. And when was the last time you had a treatment, or even needed one? That girl spent the last two week trying everything she knew to fix you, even though she had no obligation to do so. *She saved your life.* Yet you dare to look me in the face and bitch about how you were betrayed? How about you grow the fuck up?"

Sebastian tried and failed to come up with a valid response. The truth was, Willow *had* saved his life.

But that still didn't make it all better. He was still "inescapably" bound to yet another person, and it fucking killed him that even after everything he'd been through, he still had someone else magically dictating his life. And Declan still didn't get it. "If she hadn't used her magic on me—"

"You'd be dead," Declan cut in without mercy. "Or someone else would have done it and exploited the situation to the fullest instead of trying like hell to make amends."

Sebastian couldn't hope to stifle a wince at that. *I'm trying to make amends,"* Willow had said the day she'd spazzed out on wakeweed. He hadn't know what it meant then, and he wasn't sure he trusted it to mean what Declan suggested it meant.

But the seed of doubt was already sprouting roots, and that was all Declan needed. Sensing the change, he clasped his hands behind his back and said, "It might interest you to know that Willow didn't act alone."

Another sucker punch to the gut. Willow'd had an accomplice? "What…?"

"As I was about to explain before you stormed out in a fury the other night, the magical mass inside you is actually a blend of two energies."

"What the hell are you talking about?" There'd been no one else in Helegert except Willow. No way she could have smuggled in another person; they'd practically been living in each other's pockets.

The secret passageways…

Fuck, he couldn't stand this.

Declan shrugged. "Based on what you have both reported and what I have seen, it would have been impossible for Willow to fashion a binding curse in the heat of the moment. Such a spell requires massive amounts of magic, and razor-sharp focus for the duration of the spell, which is quite significant, since the subject is likely to resist. Even nonmagical people have natural defenses against the forceful removal of free will. She most definitely would not have been able to do that *and* affect Zorana's curse simultaneously."

"Unless she had help."

Declan nodded. "Indeed. For both to have happened, the magic would have to have been met and welcomed in some fashion, either magical or natural." He paused, staring at Sebastian as the implications began to sink in.

"Wait… What?"

Declan spelled it out for him. "It appears that you were a willing participant in your own healing and, since you do not possess any magic of your own, your energy, your *soul* freely entered into the fray to solidify the bond."

"You're trying to tell me I chose this." Like hell!

There was no accomplice. No deception.

I chose this.

I chose this?

"Some part of you must have. You bound her to yourself as surely as she bound you to her."

Sebastian was already shaking his head. No, it was the curse. It had to be. The kind of thing Declan described involved feelings and Sebastian didn't feel anything for Willow.

He'd admit she was beautiful and brilliant, and she'd fascinated him since the first second he'd laid eyes on her, but…

Gods, what if…?

"You should know the effects of the bond are not one-sided," Declan said in a grudgingly softer tone, "and the magic is not, shall we say, complete. Willow believes that, given the circumstances under which it came into being, a kiss might complete the magical working, but none of us have any way of predicting the result."

"So it could fix everything, or make it all a thousand times worse."

"Yes."

Sebastian sat hard on the couch. "Hell of a choice."

"It is," Declan agreed, heading for the front door. "And, curiously, Willow is determined to leave it up to you." Just like she had with her heat spell. Hardly the actions of an evil manipulator.

"Declan," Sebastian called. The footsteps stopped. "How is she?"

There was a small pause before Declan opened the door, tossing over his shoulder, "Her life as she knew it is over. How do you think she is?"

CHAPTER 18

Char av Issaven -
[extinct]

A mysterious, magical people recorded to cohabit the wintry plane of Hvitlund alongside the ice fey. Rumored to possess powerful raw soul magic that needed no spells to manifest. Considered to be an invasive species with no known origin, the Issaven were driven to extinction through systematic genocide on the part of the ice fey sometime during the reign of Kjerti Ericksson II of Sturmgard.

Only anecdotal evidence survives of their existence. The most comprehensive physical description comes from the preserved journals of historian Alvinus Graemal who visited with a tribe in Sturmgard during what is considered the final era of the species:

"[The Issaven are] humanoid in appearance, but lacking any warmth of pigmentation. Individuals are distinguished by a series of intricate blue marking around the face and across the body that appear to be natural in origin and form during the maturation stage.

While the Issaven refuse to divulge their meaning, having observed similar patterns among members of a single family unit, it is my the-

ory that the markings serve as a sort of status symbol, displaying an individual's genetic lineage at first glance."

To the venerable Fehvindt the Bright av Issaven, High Sovereign and Paladin of his Char:

In the matter of your petition for political asylum in the name of your Char, numbering two score and two in all, her Majesty Queen Kjersti Ericksson II of Sturmgard has regrettably ruled in its opposition. To grant it would be in direct conflict with Sturmgard's recently negotiated truce with Chronroth of the ice fey delegation. Her Majesty wishes to convey her deepest sympathies for your struggles and offers supplies and an armed envoy to escort the Char safely to neutral territory in the White Plains.

With humble regards,
Royal Chancellor Heinrich Dorme

A vague encyclopedic entry and the facsimile of an official document dated three days before Alvina's act of open rebellion made up the sum total of Willow's origins. She could recite it all from memory by now, and every word of it broke her heart.

"Will there be anything else, my lady?"

Willow looked away from the pages in front of her and met the stylist's smiling gaze in the vanity mirror. The woman had spent an hour arranging Willow's hair into a sleek, tight twist and looked duly proud of her achievement. "Can you get me out of dinner tonight?"

She giggled. "Not for love or money, my lady."

Willow sighed. "Didn't think so."

As much as she enjoyed the royal couple's company, being constantly surrounded by so many people sometimes made her wish she had a collapsing ruin of a castle to hide in.

She'd said as much to her cousin the other night in what she'd meant as a light-hearted jest.

The awkward silence afterward had killed any levity left in the room.

To his credit, King Marcus had responded with infinite grace—and some obvious reluctance—offering to rebuilt Helegert for her, if she wanted to go back.

It had been a moment of revelation for Willow. She'd realized then and there that the connection she'd always felt with Helegert was gone. Did she miss her home? Absolutely. Every single day. But she no longer felt a desperate need to return to it. In fact, Willow felt liberated and relieved to be free of her lifelong duty to it, which was a novel experience for her, in and of itself.

But far more monumental had been the realization that she was not only welcome, but wanted here in Kesteran. She had a family; a new place to belong. She wasn't alone anymore.

And so, with tears stinging her eyes, she'd smiled at her cousin, thanked him for his offer, and politely declined it. "If you tire of my company," she'd told him, "I'll settle in a cozy little cottage somewhere on the edge of town and never bother you again. But I like this southern sunshine far too much to ever return to the snow again."

"I heard their Majesties invited every house of nobility and note," the stylist said, bringing her back to her present dilemma. "The dining hall is set for *four hundred* of Valefort's most sought-after guests!"

"That's what I'm afraid of," Willow muttered as the stylist swept out the door.

Their Majesties had gone to a great deal of trouble for Willow's first public appearance. It was a great honor, to be sure, but Willow still felt like a dancing bear about to be put on display.

She pushed back from the vanity and faced the floor length mirror. An elegant, composed stranger with doll-like painted features stared back at her, draped in a beautiful silk gown of deep blue and silver, not a thread out of place. "Who are you?" she whispered.

It wasn't a rhetorical question. Tonight's dinner was actually a formal court affair at which Queen Snow would announce Willow's identity to the world at large and welcome her into the royal fold. And for that, Willow needed to give her a name.

She tilted her head and turned to the side to see herself in profile. "Markise Willow Ericksson." No, that didn't sound right. Nor did it sit well after Queen Kjersti had, apparently, sent Willow's forefather and all his people to their deaths in exile.

Making a face, she turned to the other side. "Princess Willow av Issaven." The words rolled off the tongue quite nicely, but what claim did she have to the name? And what would it mean for Valefort's relations with the ice fey if a blood relation to the crown took the name of the ice fey's enemy?

Willow huffed and faced forward again. "Lady Willow Faithblade." The name she'd been born to. The name a noble nobody, a ghost haunting a castle ruin—which no longer existed. Her throat constricted until she could barely breathe. "For goodness sake. What a time to have an identity crisis."

An authoritative knock admitted the young herald in training. "Master Sebastian Collins," he announced.

Willow whirled around, heart in her throat as Sebastian stepped into the room, dressed in an all-white uniform. He looked utterly beautiful, standing there at attention, and a thought of pure madness flitted across her mind: *Lady Willow Collins.*

But Sebastian wouldn't look at her. His jaw was set his posture tense, and his hands curled into fists, as if he'd rather march into battle than face her. Willow swallowed past the lump in her throat. There were so many things she wanted to say, but none of them made any difference in this impossible situation, and the chaos of them all crowding inside her brain kept her from vocalizing a simple hello.

When the silence stretched long, Sebastian cleared his throat. "The Rebels were summoned to dinner tonight. In the interest of forestalling any unpleasantness and gossip, I propose we get this over with before we go down there."

"T-that sounds reasonable." Willow frowned. "What exactly are we getting over with?"

"Declan told me about your theory. And you should know he's waiting outside to confirm the results of whatever happens."

"I see."

He hadn't moved an inch, not even a glance in her general direction. The tether between them was so taut it hummed under the immense strain of a "push" of resistance that now accompanied its original pull, rendering it almost inert. Considering how powerful she knew that pull to be, the strength of Sebastian's fight had to be at least as powerful.

He hated her.

And Willow couldn't blame him.

"Well?" Sebastian finally looked her way, and his eyes widened as he stared at her.

Willow flushed. Needing something to do with her hands, she reached up to adjust her glasses only to remember she was wearing contact lenses. Oh, she hated when people stared! Under normal circumstances, she'd leave the room, or hide behind a task of some sort, but neither was an option at the moment. Instead, she retreated into the safety of her theory's magical minutiae. "The procedure should be fairly simple. I don't believe any embellishments to be necessary. It's a symbolic gesture, more than anything, but then there's never anything simple in the mingling of breath and life, is there—"

"Take it down."

"I beg your pardon?"

"Your hair. Take it down."

Willow reached up to the neat twist nestled at her nape. "No." Someone had finally managed to get her hair to behave; Willow was not about to undo an hour of hard work and not a small amount of pain on a whim.

Sebastian's mouth compressed into a frustrated line. "It isn't you."

"What are you talking about?"

In answer, Sebastian strode straight for her.

"What are you doing? Stop it!" She tried to bat away his hands, but it was too late. With a few quick tugs, he removed enough pins for her hair to break free of the rest of them and cascade down her back. All that effort utterly undone. And the dinner started in fifteen minutes. Willow wanted to cry. She shoved against his chest, making him step back. "Why did you do that?"

Sebastian didn't answer. He seemed beyond words, staring at her with something like awe. She flinched when he raised his hand again, and he winced, pausing with his hand suspended in the air between them. But he wasn't deterred. He reached out slowly, catching a skein of her hair and bringing it forward. The second time, he smoothed the strands between his fingers from her temple down to the tips. On his third pass, his knuckles brushed down her cheek, and his fingers came to rest ever so lightly on the side of her throat.

"I didn't mean to curse you," she said with all the volume of a whisper.

"I know," Sebastian replied, then met her gaze and repeated, "I *know*." But despite the conviction in those words, a painful uncertainty still remained in his gaze. The truth was, he *wouldn't* know until the tether between them was severed. If it even could be severed.

They stood so close together Willow's skirt brushed Sebastian's legs. The sun's final rays made his uniform all but glow, casting him in loving golden light that brought out the green in his eyes, and for the briefest of moments, Willow didn't want the kiss to work.

She was just selfish enough that she didn't want to watch Sebastian walk out of her life forever. She didn't want to become stuck in this beautiful place where she would see him every day as nothing but a stranger, and speak to him in short, formal exchanges, and eventually watch him fall in love and marry someone else.

How am I any different than the woman who cursed him in the first place?

Sebastian's throat worked on a swallow. Willow felt a minute tremor in his hand where it rested against her skin. Her own hands clutched at her skirts, wrinkling the smooth fabric beyond repair, but she really had no other choice. If she let go, Sebastian would be the only thing for her to hold onto, and she might never release him again. "Shall we, then?" she prompted, needing him to move, to get this over with, as he'd said, before she lost her nerve.

Sebastian nodded as the tip of his tongue speared out to wet his lips before he leaned toward her. He hesitated a hair's breadth from full contact, huffing a soft sigh against her lips, and Willow shivered as she felt his resistance slowly break down, reviving the tether to its full, inescapable strength.

And then his mouth pressed against hers, his nose brushed alongside hers. Willow forced herself to hold still and resist the compulsion to deepen the kiss, to steal just one more taste of him so she'd have something to remember him by.

The magical tether flared brighter, hotter, pulling tighter than it ever had until she felt Sebastian against her from chest to hip. The height difference between them meant she had to tilt her head back to maintain contact and she was grateful when Sebastian's arm came around her waist to hold her steady. His other hand speared farther into her hair, cradling her nape as he moved his mouth over hers, opening his lips enough to catch at hers, and Willow's need turned desperate.

It's the magic, she told herself, even as she looped her arms around Sebastian and held on for all she was worth; savored every moment of the sweetest kiss she'd ever had and would ever get; committed every detail to her memory so she'd have something to hold her heart together as it broke.

It wasn't just the magic. Not anymore. What Willow felt reached deeper, to a place beyond magical influence, and it felt like truth. *I want you,* she acknowledged. *I want you to want me. But if this is all you can ever give me, I'll never ask for more.*

The tether's pull suddenly gave, arcing up and out, twisting and coiling until it formed a searing hot circle above their heads that dropped down around them and burst in a glorious, blinding fireworks display Sebastian would never see.

When it cleared at last, and Sebastian pulled back to search her gaze, Willow had to remind herself to breathe. She focused her sight on the center of his chest. "H-how do you feel?" she asked, trying to make sense of what she was seeing.

"You tell me," he returned. His entire body was tense as if bracing for a physical blow, but his arms were still around her, as unwilling to release her as Willow was to let go of him.

With great reluctance, she freed one hand to hover it over his chest so she could feel the result of their kiss. "There's still magic in you," she confessed. "It's rooted deep, and I don't think I can pull it out.

B-but it seems to be…inert. It's not doing anything that I can sense."

"You're certain?"

The urgency of Willow's aching need had abated, but she still craved Sebastian more than her next breath.

Was she certain? No. Not in the least.

But she owed it to him to be certain. So she reached out to the pulsing nest of magic with her own. It felt familiar, but different at the same time, almost like a mirror image of herself.

Willow forgot to breathe. That was precisely what it was: a part of her gift, integrated into his being. It stretched to his heart, his lungs, his brain, and all through the rest of his body like an auxiliary neural network made of magic, but it wasn't affecting him. If anything, it felt like it was awaiting his command.

Willow tried to bind the core of it the way she'd done with his curse, and it expelled her so violently it physically pushed her back away from Sebastian.

Sebastian caught hold of her arms and righted her before she could tip over. "What the hell was that?"

Shaking her head as if to clear it, Willow dazedly reached out to him again, doing that maddening non-touch thing that still drove him up the fucking wall. "What did it feel like?" she asked with a quiver in her voice. Whatever it had felt like to him, it had hurt *her*.

"I don't know," he said, trying and failing to catch her gaze. She was focused on his chest again, but her hand shook and her breath was unsteady.

"Any pain?"

"No." Not in the usual sense, anyway. The bone-grinding agony was gone. Even the beehives in his bones had disappeared. But he still ached like a son of a bitch, and that sweet, chaste kiss they'd just shared had only made him want her more. The static of her non-touch now reached deep into him, and he felt like he'd lose his fucking mind if she didn't make physical contact.

"Any driving urges that feel out of character?"

What's out of character? "I don't know."

Finally, she frowned up at him. "What does that mean?"

In answer, he covered her hand with one of his and pressed it firmly to his chest, stifling a shudder of pleasure at her touch, even through the layers of his uniform. Sebastian couldn't stop there. Pulling her close again, he kissed her the way he'd been aching to for days, pouring out all his frustration into her, taking hers in return. He could taste her surprise on his tongue, and delved deeper, again and again, savoring each shift and sway.

Willow didn't relax into his hold; she latched onto him and kissed him back with a fervor that made him weak in the knees and nothing, absolutely nothing had ever felt that good before. Her hands clutched at his hair, her leg came up to his hip, and Sebastian burned beneath the onslaught of pure, unadulterated lust.

He picked her up so she could put both legs around him. Hindered by her skirts, she only managed to get halfway there, but it was still more than enough. It told Sebastian that, even with all the magics stripped away, Willow still wanted him as much as he did her.

You don't know that, doubt whispered.

Yes, I do. Sebastian might not understand exactly *how* he knew, but he did. Somehow, he'd felt that artificial connection to Willow break during their kiss. And that awareness was still there. Sebastian perceived his entire being, inside and out, and he could feel there was nothing forcing him toward Willow anymore, aside from his own desire for her.

In that moment, closed away in a frilly pink room with the entire castle bustling outside the door, it was just the two of them. The spectre of Zorana's evil that had haunted him his entire life was finally gone, exorcised by Willow's goodness and tenacity, and a faery tale kiss Sebastian would never forget as long as he lived.

He clutched her tighter, kissed her deeper, savoring the feel of her against his body, the taste of her on his tongue, and the scrape of her nails on his skull. There was a bed in here, wasn't there? He was almost certain he'd glimpsed one when he'd come in.

Yes! There, across the room. Sebastian turned to head for it, but stopped short when his phone emitted a series of loud, high-pitched beeps. He broke the kiss, buried his face in Willow's shoulder and tried to tell himself it was nothing.

Just to be contrary, his phone beeped again.

"Do you need to get that?" Willow asked, breathing hard, in no hurry to let go of him.

"Probably," Sebastian said, in no hurry to fish the phone out of his pocket.

"They'll be waiting for us at dinner."

Sebastian didn't like that. He still had an obligation to the crown and Willow, as the guest of honor, couldn't just decide not to show. Like it or not, both of them were expected to make an appearance, and soon.

He growled and pressed Willow's back against one of the bedposts for leverage so he could retrieve his damned phone without setting her down. The screen was lit up with two received text messages. The first one was from Declan:

CAME IN 2 CHECK U OUT. U WERE BUSY.
KISS WORKED. CONGRATS. REALLY.

Sebastian grinned at that. *Your bedside manner still sucks, buddy.* But he appreciated the sentiment and, even though he didn't need it anymore, he was grateful for an unbiased confirmation as well.

The second message was from Marcus:

SENDING STYLIST BACK. EXPECT U BOTH
DOWN HERE & PRESENTABLE IN 30 MINS.

He was about to reply that they'd be there when another message came through:

AND WE WILL B DISCUSSING
UR INTENTIONS W/ MY COUSIN. FYI.

"Why are you scowling?" Willow asked.

LOOKING FWD 2 TELLING U 2 FUK OFF, Sebastian typed out and hit Send before he changed his mind. "No reason. Marcus is sending the stylist back. We have thirty minutes to get our asses down to dinner."

Willow appeared to consider that. "I'll only need about ten, and the dining hall is five minutes away, which leaves fifteen. That's a lot of extra time."

"It is."

"Whatever shall we do with it?"

Sebastian grinned. "I'm sure we'll come up with something."

They never made it down to dinner.

Happily, neither of them cared.

Afterword

Dear reader,

Alvina Ericksson might not have left any clues about her secret lover, but their story is still a significant part of Willow's heritage, and one worth including, even in this limited form.

Alvina's mystery lover was Fehvind the Bright himself, one of a forgotten people whose unique gift was soul magic. Willow's theory about her forefather's gift affecting her own was right on the money—she never could have fully removed Sebastian's curse without it. But she was wrong about having accidentally created a new one in the process. Even soul magic cannot create an artificial connection; it can only build upon what already exists. In Willow and Sebastian's case, it amplified their natural fascination for one another and made it impossible to ignore until they both acknowledged it was real. What remained afterward was a part of Willow's gift shared with Sebastian the same way Ericksson women had been sharing their magic with their menfolk throughout history.

But back to Alvina and Fehvind.

The couple met and fell in love during a week-long royal audience in Sturmgard where Fehvind presented his people's petition for political asylum to the queen. Their soul connection was so powerful that, when Fehvind and his people were forced to depart, Alvina chose to follow him to White Plains, rather than continue living without him in Sturmgard.

Sadly, that is where their tale turned tragic.

Relentlessly pursued by the murderous ice fey warriors, the last surviving Issaven made their final stand in Helegert Castle at the height of the human Battle of White Plains. As the ice fey launched their assault, tearing the castle apart, Fehvind the Bright realized that his people's lives were already forfeit, but Alvina and her child might still have a chance—if the fight could be ended before her pregnancy was discovered.

Alas, the only way to make that happen was to let the ice fey win. Despite Alvina's wretched protests, the *char* decided to make the ultimate sacrifice for the sake of their legacy. They gave up their physical bodies turning themselves into pure energy which soaked into the castle's stone walls, along with their very souls so that their combined energy could keep the castle standing and safeguard its inhabitants for as long as one of their own was in residence.

It worked. Sensing the Issaven's dissolution, the ice fey retreated, leaving the pregnant Alvina alone in the Helegert ruin, surrounded by the essence of her husband and his people, and forever isolated from the outside world.

The Battle of White Plains ended shortly thereafter in a victory for Valefort, and went down in history as the only human battle in which the ice fey ever took part.

No mention of the Issaven or their disappearance was ever made.

I hope you enjoyed reading Sweetest Kiss as much as I enjoyed writing it.

Until next time!

Alianne

About the Author

Alianne Donnelly was a wordsmith long before she became a reader. Driven by an insatiable curiosity about everything from history and mythology to science and philosophy, she grew into a fiction writer who hates coloring inside the genre lines. Her books all have elements of romance, with different series sorted under paranormal, science fiction, fantasy, and erotic. And then there's *Wolfen*…

Alianne lives in California, doing hard time in a corporate 9-5, while secretly scribbling away any chance she gets. She loves pizza, hiking, and avoiding small talk, and hopes to one day win the lottery jackpot.

www.ingramcontent.com/pod-product-compliance
Lightning Source LLC
Chambersburg PA
CBHW051703180726
48283CB00004B/1198